Flora Macdonald Macdonald

The Autobiography of Flora M'Donald

Vol. II

Flora Macdonald Macdonald

The Autobiography of Flora M'Donald
Vol. II

ISBN/EAN: 9783337013530

Printed in Europe, USA, Canada, Australia, Japan

Cover: Foto ©Raphael Reischuk / pixelio.de

More available books at **www.hansebooks.com**

THE

AUTOBIOGRAPHY

OF

FLORA M'DONALD

BEING

The Home Life of a Heroine

EDITED BY HER GRAND-DAUGHTER

"The preserver of Prince Charles Edward Stuart will be mentioned in history, and if courage and fidelity be virtues, mentioned with honour."
—DOCTOR JOHNSON.

IN TWO VOLUMES—VOL. II.

Second Edition.

EDINBURGH
WILLIAM P. NIMMO
1870

AUTOBIOGRAPHY

OF

FLORA M'DONALD.

———◇———

IT was now the beginning of September. For two whole dreary months had I been a prifoner; but it was not fo much that fact which at times weighed on my mind, as the ftate of uncertainty regarding the Prince's movements, joined to the knowledge of my dear old friend Kingfburgh's being at that moment confined in Fort Auguftus, thrown into a damp dungeon, loaded with irons! And if his poor wife fhould hear of it! My heart bled for her mifery. Really, but for knowing all this, and being fo far from home, I fhould have been comfortable enough; and truly did it aftonifh me to have to receive

Prifon.

A lion.

ladies and gentlemen who actually came on board to fee—whom do you fuppofe, dear Maggie?—my ain fimple Highland felf! I was made a fight of as being "The Prince's Preferver," which was a name I liked to hear from the Jacobite ladies; but others of a different way of thinking ftigmatifed me as "The fair rebel who had faved the Pretender's life." So there were daily crowds of people flocking to fee the wonderful Mifs M'Donald! How filly all this was! It was really abfurd. Yet fome were very kind, making me nice pretty prefents as remembrances of their vifiting me on board the fhip, and ufeful articles too. Plenty of threads and needles came for Katie, and a lady brought a Bible and Book of Prayer, which delighted me very much, not having been able to procure for myfelf a copy of God's bleffed Word fince leaving home. I did, indeed, more than ever need its daily perufal, fo ftrengthening and confoling are its holy promifes at any time, but more efpecially in the hour of trial and diftrefs.

Some of the lady vifitors came fo often, that Captain Knowler told me I was perfectly welcome to offer them refrefhments, or even invite them to dine with me, if I wifhed.

And now I muft mention an amufing fact. On one occafion Lady Mary Cochrane, who frequently vifited me, had come to pafs the day on board, and a breeze fpringing up, fhe requefted leave to remain the night, being afraid of a fmall boat in fuch a high wind. She afferted this as the reafon, but what, think you, was her fly motive? I really, although fo long ago, can fcarcely fummon courage to ftate what may be confidered, from my pen, a piece of vanity. There being no other ladies' cabin, of courfe fhe fhared mine, and while we were preparing for reft, fhe confeffed her fole defire for remaining on board was a wifh to be able to tell her

Fancy.

friends, that fhe had flept in the fame bed with Mifs Flora M'Donald.

Now, to explain this, I muft tell you, Maggie, I had obtained leave to have the comfort of a bedftead, fmall as it was, in my cabin ; for being fo long a time in the fhip, it would have greatly added to my difcomfort to have been obliged to ufe the narrow bedding, mounted on a kind of fhelf, which was called a berth, for a continuance. So I boldly afked for a proper bed, and got it. But for this, Lady Mary would certainly not have been able to obtain her wifh. Oh, how I laughed at fuch nonfenfe ! Yet this aĉt was trifling to the flattering notice I received at a later period.

The vifitors frequently ftayed until late in the evening, when fometimes they managed to have a dance, and feemed furprifed when I declined joining. Ah ! they could not guefs the heavy heart concealed under many a forced fmile ! Had I not caufe to feel fad, when often, in the midſt of their merriment, the thought would riſe uppermoſt, that moſt probably all I had done was, after ſo much riſk, of no avail?

One day I was made miſerable by a young gentleman accompanying ſome ladies coming on deck with the—to me—diſaſtrous intelligence of Prince Charles being taken by a militia troop in Moidart, and it was not until the next day that the idle report was contradicted.

Alſo the name of Malcolm M'Leod catching my ear, I was fair grieved to know he was a priſoner on board a ſloop then bound   *Another.* for London. It was ſome time before I had the opportunity of hearing particulars of his capture, which was almoſt immediately after he took leave of the Prince, after having conducted his Royal Highneſs · to Ellagol, the houſe of his brother-in-law, John M'Kinnon. The Prince was much affected, I was told, on parting from Malcolm, gave him his ſilver ſhoe-buckles, and warmly embraced him;

and he put ten guineas into his hand, which the
Captain ftoutly refufed, fufpecting the purfe
they came from was not too heavily filled;
but the Prince affured him he had more than
would be required while on the Mainland,
and obliged him to accept the money. His

The pipe.

Royal Highnefs gave Malcolm the pipe he
was fmoking, which, I heard in later years,
has been preferved in a fhagreen cafe, and is
in the poffeffion of another fellow prifoner,
Doctor Burton of York.

And while all this unhappy news was
worrying my mind, I was expected to play
the agreeable to many ftrangers, who were
defignated by the fhip's officers as Mifs
M'Donald's guefts. I had no objection to
fing a few of my fimple Highland ditties,
which they were feemingly pleafed with; but
as for exerting myfelf by dancing, I could not
and would not, and when preffed almoft beyond the verge of politenefs, I fpoke out
boldly :—" My dancing for the prefent, under

the circumftances in which I am placed, is out of the queftion, for I am too anxious about the Prince's fafety, and that of my near relations and friends, to be able to divert myfelf in any way." The rebellious tears ftarted to my eyes while thus fpeaking, and fome of the ladies expreffed fympathy for me; indeed, there were a few for whom I began to entertain a fincere liking, but the many came to ftare at me, as if I had been a wild animal juft exported from the Blue Mountains.

At laft, to my joy, *The Bridgewater* was put under failing orders for London. She left Leith Roads the 7th November, and reached the Nore on the 28th; and as poor Katie and I were to be tranfferred to another veffel, Commodore Smith and Captain Knowler took a moft kind leave of me, expreffing their hope of all going well, and of my foon being at liberty. They alfo promifed to fpeak in my favour to parties high in office, but whether they did exert their influence or not, I never heard.

The Nore.

Well, now behold us on board another fhip, *The Royal Sovereign* — a compliment, I imagined, to him who was filling the place of Prince Charlie's royal father, which fovereign was foft Geordie of Hanover. However, I would not vex myfelf by thinking of what fhould have been. No indeed; my thoughts were otherwife taken up, for it muft be confeffed, I felt nervous on hearing from the converfation around, it was fully expeéted I fhould be imprifoned in the for-

Gloom.

trefs of London, the difmal dark Tower about which I had been accuftomed to read from childhood, and at home we had a large engraving of it hanging in the room where we took our daily leffons.

How ftrange are the viciffitudes of life! Little did I formerly think the day would arrive when I fhould be incarcerated in fuch a gloomy place, and poffibly landed in a boat at the ftairs of the Traitors' Gate!

It was on the 6th December, a cold, raw

day (as cold as my poor heart was), when we were taken to London and lodged in the Tower. I fay we, becaufe honeſt Katie was more my friend and companion than my ſervant.

It being late in the evening when we arrived, the effect of the dark ſhadows thrown on the time-worn walls of the dreaded maſſy pile of ſtonework was gloomy indeed, and equally gloomy were the ſad reflections of the lonely Highland laſſie, who then began to realiſe the probability of loſing her life.

Yes; it was more than probable I might never again paſs thoſe ſtern, forbidding-looking portals until on the way to a ſcaffold!

But not a queſtion would I aſk, or betray the leaſt ſign of fear, while following the warders to the rooms aſſigned to "Flora M'Donald and her perſonal attendant, a young Highland girl," for thus were we poor priſoners deſignated in a huge piece of parchment, which was read out in due form as ſoon as we had paſſed the wicket-gate of the

Firm.

portcullis. I fancied the rooms were in a private part of the building, for although very fmall and low, with high narrow windows, they were not meanly furnifhed. But enough of bolts and bars, as you may fuppofe. However, to the ufe of these unfriendly articles by that time I was pretty well accuftomed.

Dull.

Oh ! how monotonous were the hours I paffed while kept a prifoner, with few books, no wheel for fpinning, only a little needle-fewing and fpeaking Gaelic with Katie. Really, but for the companionfhip of that kind, fimple girl, I think my brain would have turned. The only relaxation we were allowed was an occafional walk in the dull old garden—at leaft in the fpot of ground they called a garden—of burnt-up grafs, and walks covered with dufky mofs and lichens.

Yet it was a change to be taken from our low rooms and to feel the air. How my heart panted for a mountain breeze ! My ftep-father would have grieved had he feen the fading cheeks of his bonnie Highland rofe! Moft fervently did I pray that the dear ones at home might be kept in ignorance of my perilous pofition.

But in the midft of fuch diftrefs, I could not be left quiet, for even a portrait-painter hunted me out, having got permiffion from the Conftable of the Tower, not only to fee me, but to requeft "the honour" of my granting him a fitting. I was very provoked, and at firft flatly refufed; but the man looked fo difappointed, and as the poor wretch had his canvas and paints ready prepared, I could but confent,—in truth, more to oblige Katie than to pleafe myfelf, for I felt much too quiet and fad to have any tranfactions with painters at that moment.

The honeft girl was quite excited on the occafion, and was rufhing to the boxes to get out a better gown than I ufually wore while in captivity, but I pofitively refufed to drefs up. "No," faid I, "the Englifh folks who

Drefs.

Picture.

fo wifh for my pale face fhall fee me juft as I am." So if hereafter a picture of my wonderful felf fhould ever be forthcoming from perhaps fome pawnbroker's fhop, of a difconfolate-looking damfel in a dark ruffet gown, with a white rofe ftuck in the hair, named on the back "Mifs Flora M'Donald, pinx. 1746," the finder will, I hope, confider he has got a treafure.

While with Lady Primrofe, at a later period, fhe infifted on my fitting to fome of the firft artifts, and then her Ladyfhip had me dreffed in grand ftyle. I really forget how often I had to undergo this penance, but at that time I was in brighter looks and fpirits than when I felt fo miferable in the gloomy Tower.

And in thinking of thofe I loved at home, ay, and of another far diftant—of that one who then filled my heart, and who was in after-years to be my own—fuch reflections made me fad. Where were they? How occupied? Poffibly longing to hear of me, without an idea of the danger I fhould have incurred by attempting to get a letter paffed through thofe difmal portals !

At laft the joyful tidings came that I was to be releafed from the Tower, and received into the houfe of a private family, who were to keep guard over me until further orders. Really, the high authorities did not appear to know how to deal with the young rebel ! Katie was now quite fure that " the daughter of her father's houfe" would ultimately efcape punifhment, return to the homeftead, and that we (for fhe always included herfelf in fuch details) fhould be moft marvellous additions to the wonders of the world !

It was indeed with a deep-drawn figh of relief that I turned my back on the dreadful fortrefs fo renowned in hiftory, but of which I had had more than enough for my experience. We were taken in a clofe coach, guarded by a troop of the Tower folk, to the gentleman's houfe, where we had comfortable

Change.

accommodation. The ladies of the family received me very courteoufly, yet without a remark as to the length of my ftay, or when I might expeƈt to be finally releafed from the Argus-eyes of my perfecutors.

It is ftrange that I have quite forgotten the name of thefe worthy people, to whom I owe a debt of gratitude for fundry little aƈts of confiderate kindnefs and forethought, knowing the awkwardnefs of my pofition while under their care.

While thus, as one might have faid, on the ladder of liberation from captivity, how was I aftonifhed to hear that I might poffibly be **Visitor.** honoured by a perfonal vifit from "His Royal Highnefs Frederick, Prince of Wales!" It appeared he had much curiofity to fee "The Pretender's Deliverer," for fuch was my defignation at the Eleƈtor's court, and had been heard to afk where I was, for he wifhed to queftion me himfelf.

Accordingly, one bright afternoon, when I

was fitting in the beft room with the lady of the houfe at our fewing-work, a plain dark-painted coach drove to the door, in which were three gentlemen. The fervants were in handfome livery coats, but there was nothing in the appearance of the equipage to denote its belonging to a perfon of confe-quence; fo, as I was in the habit of having people coming frequently to fee " Mifs Flora M'Donald," I thought thefe vifitors might be fome of them, therefore continued my occupa-tion very leifurely, when the room door was thrown widely open, and "The Prince of Wales" —alas! not my Prince—was announced.

We inftantly rofe, but in a very courteous way he begged us to refeat ourfelves, and re-quefted to know which of the ladies he was to addrefs as Mifs Flora M'Donald?

I muft tell you the lady was about my own age. He motioned to the two other gentlemen to be feated, and then turning to me, he faid, in a grave, conftrained manner—

Visit

"I am here, madam, by his Majefty's commands, it having been reprefented to him the very extraordinary courfe of conduct you have lately purfued, in having aided the efcape from Scotland of the Pretender, Charles Edward Stuart. I would afk why you have done fo, and been guilty of an act which not only involves the greateft danger to yourfelf, fhould it be his Majefty's pleafure to carry out the punifhment of treafon, the crime of which you are accufed, but alfo imperils the lives of feveral of your country-men, and I believe your relatives, who have entangled themfelves in difficulties, the effects of your rafhnefs? That fuch a young girl as you are fhould have joined in this headftrong fcheme, appears almoft incredible. And for what purpofe? Let me afk you, Mifs M'Donald, to explain the motive which induced you thus to hazard your life. When you engaged in this tranf-action, you muft have known it was an act of rebellion againſt the crown of England. I aſk you, therefore, why did you do it? what induced you to think of doing it ? "

While he was ſpeaking, I had caſt my eyes down to hide a quivering lip, for I did feel nervous when he talked of treaſon and loſing life. I felt he was looking earneſtly at me; but towards the cloſe of his addreſs, his manner and voice were leſs ſtern, which gave me courage to recover myſelf, and reply—" Your Highneſs does me injuſtice by ſuppoſing that either in thought or deed I had a deſire of aſting in any way contrary to the laws of this country; nay, it is true, and can be proved, that when it was propoſed to me to aid the Prince "—(I was determined to ſtyle my ain Charlie by his title)—" I firmly refuſed, nor was it until I ſaw the miſerable ſtate of deſtitution in which he was plunged, that I reluſtantly conſented to carry out the plan propoſed." Here he interrupted me, quickly ſaying, " Who propoſed it to you ? '

Not guilty.

True.

"I muſt reſpectfully decline anſwering that queſtion. Many, whom I know, are in trouble on account of this affair, and far be it from my lips to ſay the word that would injure them. Your Highneſs is pleaſed to aſk my motive: I ſimply followed the dictates of common humanity in endeavouring to ſave a human being from miſery,—perhaps ſtarvation. That was my ſole motive in agreeing to take him acroſs the water, and as I was going home to my mother in Sleat, the opportunity was ſeized on. I did convey him to Portree, and I am neither ſorry for it, nor aſhamed of having done ſo. If your Highneſs or any of your family had applied to me under ſimilar diſtreſſing circumſtances, I ſhould, with the bleſſing of God, have acted in the ſame manner."

He was ſilent for a few minutes, as if in deep thought, then, in a kinder manner, he ſaid, "Well, madam, I am glad to have heard your verſion of this unfortunate affair, and

from what you ſtate, it ſeems to me that your
adviſers, whoever they may have been, are
much to be blamed for having placed you in
the awkward poſition you are at preſent.
Moſt reprehenſible has been their conduct,
and when the caſe is repreſented to his
Majeſty I feel aſſured he will be of the ſame
opinion. I truſt, alſo, he may be diſpoſed to
view your conduct more leniently, yet I can
promiſe nothing." He then roſe, and addreſſing the gentlemen, who up to this moment
had ſat like two dumbies, ſaid, "Come, my
lords, we will no longer encroach on the
time of theſe ladies." They all bowed and
left the room. So much for my interview
with royalty. And juſt after the coach horſes
were heard clattering over the ſtony ſtreet,
who ſhould burſt into the room, and ruſh to me
with a kiſs of warm affection, but the beſt of
all good-hearted creatures, Lady Primroſe, a
Jacobite lady with whom I had become
acquainted ſince being releaſed from the

Acquitted.

Tower. She was one of the many who over-whelmed me with kindnefs, and continually fent gifts of every defcription. I was very fond of her, and that you may judge of her manner, her Ladyſhip ſhall fpeak for herſelf.

Liſten.

"Well, my dear foul, I am fo delighted to be the firſt to tell the news! Don't be fur-prifed, my dear, or accufe me of being a mean liftener, for I plead guilty to having hid myſelf on the ftairs while thofe Hanoverian deputies were crofs-queftioning you. Yes; and what did I hear his Royal Highnefs—for fo I fuppofe in thefe days one muft call him— fay, as he defcended the ftairs? Thefe were his words to thofe gentlemen with him—'I really never was more perplexed, for fhe evidently meant no harm to the Government; the beft plan, I think, will be to fend the young lady back to her native country.' And then, my love, he faid more, fomething about 'female courage' that I could not exactly catch. So there's a joyful hope of your foon being at liberty, you dear thing ; and then I fhall have you with me, go about everywhere, fee all the fights of London, you yourfelf being the chief fhow of the feafon. Rely on it, Geordie will let you go in a few days, for although he is always quarrelling with Prince Frederick, yet his fon has great influence over him."

This lady, the dowager Lady Primrofe of Dunnipace, was quite a leader of fafhion in the Jacobite circle, therefore fhe was defirous of having " The Prince's Preferver " to exhibit.

But I was feeling very defponding, like a caged bird panting to be free ; for fo many months had dragged themfelves flowly away, it being now July, my fpirits drooped. No tidings from home ; no means of hearing of thofe friends who were implicated equally with myfelf. It made one's blood run cold to read in the news-fheets of the frequent executions and horrible cruelties practifed towards thofe chiefs of clans and heads of families who had taken part in the unhappy

Fafhion.

Culloden battle. Alas! alas! and where was the Prince now? and were my own relations free to return home? I had no means of afcertaining their fate. However, a bright gleam of hope fhot acrofs my chequered pathway, by the announcement of a free pardon being granted me, contained in an official letter with the Government ftamp and a huge feal attached, which merely ftated that I might confider myfelf at liberty to return to Scotland.

Free.   Oh! this was joyful news! and when I could realife the fact, the firft thought uppermoft was the delight of being able to fend letters, and hear from home—dear home! which, after all the troubles I had gone through, would be more loved than ever.

Katie was almoft demented, fcreaming in Gaelic, and weeping for joy, to the amufement of the Englifh ladies of the family. Indeed, this lady and her ftep-daughter—I *wifh* I could recollect their name—as well as the gentleman of the houfe, treated me with much kindnefs. They really feemed to regret the profpect of my leaving them; but it had long been fettled, that as foon as my releafe came, I fhould go to the refidence of good Lady Primrofe.

Nor did her Ladyfhip forget my promife, for the very next day fhe came in the rumbling old family coach, rufhed up the ftair, would help Katie in putting up our things, and feemed as pleafed as a little child with a new toy.

A toy.

And thus it was that I became a refident with this worthy lady—fo kind fhe was in every way.

"And now, my dear," faid fhe, "you muft juft be candid in telling me what money you have—perhaps none?—never mind; you fhall want for nothing while with me. So I am juft looking over your wardrobe—no offence, my dear!—to fee what will be required; for with fo many of my friends and grand people coming to fee "The Prince's Preferver," indeed, my dear, I muſt have you well dreſſed.

I was obliged to acknowledge having very little left of the ſum my dear mother had ſealed up in a ſmall packet at parting, and ſlipped into my pocket ; for having been in confinement ſo long, nearly ſix months, the neceſſity of paying extra for various needful comforts had nearly exhauſted my ſmall fund, and the ſtock of wearing apparel Katie had packed in ſuch a hurry was well nigh worn out.

Her Ladyſhip turned over all my poſſeſſions, and her inveſtigation ended in the coach being ordered round, and her taking me to a faſhionable warehouſe, and ſelecting a complete outfit of every article I could poſſibly require. One piece choſen for a company-gown was the ſweeteſt thing I ever ſaw ; a ſilk ſo thick and rich, it would ſtand alone. It was a pale roſe-colour, with alternate ſtripes of green ſhaded with brown. Oh ! I loved that pretty gown beyond all the others, and have kept the remnants; they are in my boxes fomewhere.

Well, as foon as I was duly equipped, looking, as Lady Primrofe faid, like a majeftic heroine (I muft enter this nonfenfe, Maggie), I found myfelf fairly launched on the ocean of London gaiety. It was little to my tafte, for the fimple pleafures of a quiet Highland life, the cheerful enlivening bagpipe, the lively reel, and our ftrathfpey, and the gown ornamented with the frefheft and moft fragrant heather, were preferable, I thought, to the noify mufic, the ftiff formal dance they called a minuet, which began in couples, moving fo flow, one would fuppofe they were marching at a funeral, and the coftly nofegays of greenhoufe flowers the ladies either carried in their hands or adorned their enormoufly high headgear with. But thefe thoughts I kept to myfelf while appearing pleafed and happy in the grand fociety of thofe whom I might never fee again.

Auctions.

And to be in the fashion in London, the people appeared to me to live more out of their houses than in them; in the afternoon visiting, driving in their family coaches, attending sale-rooms where trumpery articles were fold by auction to the higheft bidder, fometimes really fcarcely worth taking home; for the principal part of the amufement confifted in the ladies outbidding each other, and generally amongft friends, fo that large fums of money ufed to change hands in this frivolous way, which no doubt made their hufbands very crofs. However the town ladies would, and I fuppofe ever will, contrive to have their own way. Then came the formal dinner-parties—oh! how I ufed to yawn behind my fan—and often we went to fee the play in Drury Lane, and if it chanced to be a mournful tragedy, I could not help being fo filly as to cry, it all feemed fo natural and like real life. The beft actor was Mr Garrick, and he certainly was a great man in his profeffion. Mrs Cibber alfo was wonderfully clever: thefe were the firft ftage-performers at that time. There have been feveral fince, I believe, as clever; but it is not likely I fhall ever again be in England, nor, indeed, would I, at my age, wafte my hours on fuch idle and unprofitable vanities.

Oh! then there was another evening amufement we went to fee, or rather hear—the Opera, which, Maggie, is a pretty, but very ftrange performance, and furprifed me at firft. It was a play fet to mufic, and fung as well as acted: very fine, with dazzling fhowy dreffes and fcenery. However, it was dull for me, being in the Italian language. I often wifhed myfelf away from fuch gaieties, for I could not be happy while my mind was loaded with care.

Yet my heart was relieved of a great burden in being able to receive letters from dear Scotland. All were well in my home, but I grieved fair for poor old Kingfburgh, then

Opera.

lying in Edinburgh Caftle, after having been
fet at liberty from Fort Auguftus in miftake
for another Alexander M'Donald; fo, while on
his way home, he was again taken, and treated
with much feverity. However, in about fix
weeks from this time, he was difcharged in
the fame manner as myfelf, without a queftion
being afked.

Alas! fome of the chiefs fuffered fad lofs.

Fires. Lochiel's houfe at Auchnacary was burnt about
the end of May; Kinlochmoidart's, Keppoch's,
Glengary's, Cluny's, and Glengyle's, properties
were alfo laid in afhes. Cattle, fheep, and
goats were driven off; and, dreadful to relate,
poor people, men, women, and their bairns,
found dead on the hills, fuppofed to have
been ftarved !

The worthy lady I was with had loft a near
relation, who was executed at ·Carlifle, Sir
Archibald Primrofe of Dunnipace. She felt
it acutely at the time, yet her zeal for the
Stuarts was fo deep-rooted, that fhe faid one

day, while difcourfing on the fubject, although he had been a dearly-loved member of her family, yet for Prince Charles, had ten been facrificed, fhe could have borne the forrow.

Lady Primrofe was never tired of hearing anecdotes connected with Prince Charles, for whom I really believe fhe would have fhed her heart's blood.

I remember one day in particular, when there was a wee pig on the dinner-table, fhe caught a fmile on my countenance. "Now, Flora, I will know your thoughts—of what are you thinking, dear child? Something about a pig I am fure—come, let me hear!"

The pig.

"And pleafed you will be, dear Lady Primrofe; for that difh, of which I affure you I intend to partake, reminds me of what the Prince faid when alluding to his royal mother; and fancy, dear Lady Primrofe, until he told me, I was not aware of her having been the King of Poland's grand-daughter."

"Oh, you ignorant thing! Well, never mind. What about the Queen and the pig?"

I then related that while on our wanderings, a large fat pig ran out againſt us with ſuch a grunt as never was the like. The Prince burſt out a laughing, and after having indulged in an imitation of its melodious sound, and giving a pull at the flopping frill of his cap, which action highly amuſed me, he ſaid, "Whenever I meet one of thoſe animals, I always take off my hat (bleſs me! I forget this Betty Burke cap!) for the ſake of my dear ſainted mother, who uſed to call me her pretty pig. This was in conſequence of my having ſeen, when quite a child, a huge boar's head as a centrepiece at a court banquet, when, in preference to all the nice ſweets and rich diſhes handed round, I ſcreamed out, loud enough for all the princes, lords, and ladies, and other grand people to hear, 'Give me ſome piggy! I will have ſome piggy!'"

Squeaking.

which of courſe cauſed a general laugh at the
little Prince's childiſh folly.

"Thank you, Flora! I am glad my roaſted
favourite has been the means of my hearing
another anecdote connected with our dear
Prince. But really you ought to have
known that his mother was the Princeſs
Clementina, a grand-daughter of the depoſed
John Sobieſki. Ay, and that reminds me of ·Sobieſki.·
two valuable portraits you ſhall ſee in the
houſe of a friend of mine, of the Prince's father
and mother, painted by Sir Peter Lely. He
was a firſt-rate artiſt, and knighted by
Charles II., having gained the king's favour
by painting all the good-for-nothing ladies of
of the court. Oh, my dear! they were very
wicked in thoſe days!"

"And, Lady Primroſe, the Prince told me
another circumſtance about his mother, which
I will try to repeat in his own words—'My
mother,' he said, 'was ſuch a zealous Catholic
—nay, if it is not undutiful to her memory to

Bigot.

ufe the word, I would fay, fhe was bigoted to
that creed, in which I and my brother were
brought up. Perhaps,' he faid with a figh,
'had it been otherwife, and that I could in confcience, Mifs M'Donald, have embraced the
Proteftant faith, I might not have been in my
prefent difaftrous condition.' After this remark, he was very grave for a few minutes,
and then, with the natural livelinefs of manner
fo peculiar to himfelf, and which never
entirely forfook him, even when under the
heavieft misfortune, he turned the converfation. Oh! how I have longed for more of his
fociety, to have heard from himfelf of his
early life, of his companions, of his royal
parents, and the general habits of the country
in which he was born and educated. But,
really, while going about in fuch a fcrambling
manner, every moment in dread of difcovery,
it was impoffible to converfe freely."

"You may well fay that, my dear; and
Charlie muft have been juft a charming

creature when superbly dressed, as he always was at the court of the French King. But never mind; your adventure with him has made you a true illustration of a riddle I met with lately;—now attend:

The two first letters are   *male.*

The three first   .   .   .   *female.*

The first four   .   .   .   a brave *man.*

The whole word   .   .   a brave *woman.*

And that's what you are, dear Flora," and she kissed me,—"a *hero*ine!"

"But now, in return for your interesting stories about Charlie—mind you give me some more nice recollections—I will tell you what I heard to-day about that little crooked Scotch nobleman, Lord K——, who is famed in London for being the greatest owl in the world. He was saying to Lady Dermot that there were offices established in Scotland where every Scotchman was obliged to apply for a passport before leaving his country, and to undergo a fatiffactory examination as to his intellect, education, and fo forth, otherwife it could not be obtained ; and that the perfon was fent back, even a fecond or third time, until he reached the required ftandard of abilities. 'Then I am fure,' replied Lady Dermot, ' that when your Lordfhip left Scotland for other countries, you muft have been metamor-phofed, poffibly caged, as the bird of wifdom.' Capital idea, was it not ?   I fuppofe poor Lord K—— will never open his mouth again in Lady Dermot's drawing-room."

Air.

While ftaying with Lady Primrofe I had few opportunities of enjoying country air and exercife, which young people require if only for health's fake.   Her Ladyfhip was very thoughtful in this refpect, confiding me to the care of an elderly perfon, who was a kind of female factotum in the family, moft thoroughly truftworthy, and a native of the Weft Highlands.   When on our walking-excurfions, Katie accompanied me, but Mrs

Dale was needed to efcort us, for we did not know the neighbourhood of London.

An adventure happened to me while on one of thefe expeditions, when we wandered through a pretty village into a retired lane leading to a wood. A pair of country lovers were feated on a ruftic bench, too much intent on themfelves to hear our footfteps on the foft grafs.

"What! deceive you, dear Phœbe? I would tear my bafe heart out firft! No; all will foon be fettled, for father will give me a few pounds a year, fo with my daily work, which you know is paid every week, dear love, we fhall do very well. Never fear! I love you too dearly ever to forget you. Father fays the lord of the manor has lowered his rent and granted a new leafe, and the fteward is to call to-morrow to fettle it all."

The poor girl looked up in his face, a tear gliftening like a dewdrop. "O William!

how happy you make me ! how kind of the good gentleman! We muft be grateful in thanking the worthy fteward for managing it fo well."

Blufhes.

At this moment Phœbe faw our party, fo fhe rofe up, giving William a nudge to notice our approach, and fhe dropped a bobbing courtefey, juft as the Prince had done not long before, while the lad jumped up, with a hafty pull at his hair in country fafhion.

I entered into their interefting little love profpeêts and family hiftory, faying I wifhed them fuccefs, and fhould come again in a few days to make further inquiries after them. Katie, who always had a word on any fubjeêt where her miftrefs was concerned, fcreamed out, as we continued our walk, "Ay ! and wouldna the good leddy at hame" (Lady Prim-rofe) "gie ye fome gear for houfe-warming ? Ye'll mak' a bonnie pair, though ye're likely, I ween, to ha'e mair luve in the heart than filler in the purfe." Now, this being ex-

preffed by honeft Katie in Gaelic, the poor
peafants ftared with eyes and mouths wide
open at hearing a jargon in an unintelligible
language, which Mrs Dale gave them the
meaning of, in a more fubdued voice than
Katie made ufe of.

A few days after, on returning to the
village, the whole afpect of the lovers' bright
hopes had changed, and it was with difficulty
I could make out poor Phœbe's fimple tale,
owing to the fobs which burft from her heart
on meeting us again. It feemed that the falfe
fteward had his own views in perfuading his
mafter to act kindly by the farmer's family.
He was in love with pretty Phœbe, who
indignantly rejected his difhonourable offers,
which he afcribed to her partiality for
William; and he had fpitefully told falfe tales
of the family, which induced the lord of the
manor to order them off his property; added
to which, a recruiting-party being in the
village, he had taken means to have poor

Clouds.

William decoyed into the ale-houſe, well plied with drink, and given the ſhilling for being enliſted. Fancy poor Phœbe's diſtreſs on ſeeing the gay ribbons in the hat of her lover, and the agony of her mind greatly in-creaſed by his upbraiding her for having liſtened to the worthleſs ſteward. She madly aſſured him of her innocence, went on her knees to the corporal to try to buy him off with all the money ſhe poſſeſſed, a miſerable eight ſhillings, but a guinea was required.

Tears.

She told her ſtory ſo pathetically, I believe I dropped a tear, and as for Katie, ſhe blubbered aloud, vowing vengeance on the gentleman and his overſeer. My hand was in my pocket. I gave her the guinea, and good Mrs Dale added her trifle.

The name of the lieutenant in command was given to me. Strange to ſay I knew him, for he viſited Lady Primroſe; ſo I took an opportunity to intereſt him in the affair, and he kindly ſent William home, when, after a meeting with Phœbe, the lovers were reconciled, everything explained, and they were very foon married ; not, however, before they had kiffed my hands in gratitude.

There is a great delight in being inftrumental to the happinefs of our fellow-beings, in whatever path of life they may move in. Lady Primrofe affifted them in furnifhing their little cottage, and I have often inquired after the welfare of my ruftic couple.

Believe me, dear Maggie, my life while in England was not exactly an uneventful one. I can inftance a circumftance that occurred while I was with Lady Primrofe. She had country friends about fifty miles from London, Sir Archibald and Lady B——, with whom, from fo conftantly meeting, and their uniform kindnefs, I felt myfelf on intimate terms.

Events.

They were not Scotch, but they were fo bit by the Jacobite mania, that all affairs connected with the bonnie Prince were regarded with peculiar intereft, which alfo made me come in for a larger fhare of their admiration than fuch a fimple Highland laffie would otherwife have merited. To reach their refidence, it was ufual to take the daily coach, a public conveyance holding four infide and eight on the roof. True, I might have gone to the expenfe of a pofting-carriage, and, as matters turned out, I devoutly wifhed I had ; but how happy it is for us that we cannot forefee events and probable dangers !

Alone.

Katie did not accompany me on my vifit to Highton Park, for really her ftrange ways and noife amongft Lady B———'s fafhionable airified English fervants, would have made me very uncomfortable, fo I determined to take the journey alone. Lady Primrofe faw me to the coach, and my only fellow-traveller was a young man of elegant appearance, with a gentle, pleafing countenance. I fmiled farewell to Lady Primrofe, the footman faw my box placed on the roof, and the coach rattled on.

My young gentleman was moſt polite, raiſed and lowered the windows to ſuit my convenience, and after a while entered into a moſt agreeable converſation reſpecting foreign countries and habits. He had a travelling book in his hand, the leaves of which being uncut, he uſed a paper-knife. Maggie, you have ſeen the kind of knife a hundred times, an ivory cutter, with penknife at the end. Oh! how well I remember that knife!

Well, all went on ſmoothly, and might perhaps have continued ſo, had I not made a very natural, yet, as it turned out, a moſt un-fortunate remark. "Sir," ſaid I, "you appear to have been a great traveller." No ſooner were thoſe words ſaid, than he raiſed his hands in a moſt excited way, almoſt ſhouting out, "Traveller! yes, indeed, I have been a traveller! and for what, madam? Tell me why, and for what cause I have travelled, madam?" Here he motioned nearer to me, at the ſame time flouriſhing the cutter with

The ſpring.

its open blade.—" For my health, yes; madam, for the recovery of my health from a brain fever. They faid I was out of my mind, mad for fome time; but that was a lie, I was foon as well as I am now."—He laughed in that dreadfully idiotic way fo peculiar to

infanity.—" I am quite recovered—as well as ever I was. You fee I am quite well. Tell me directly you do not doubt it. Tell me fo." And then he ftarted up, catching hold of my wrift, while his eyes glared like a wild bull. Oh! how alarmed I was! in fact I was too frightened to fcream, and had I done fo, perhaps he would have ufed his knife. My heart beat to that degree, I could hear its pulfations. I dreaded the weapon being plunged into me. " You don't think me mad! Say you fee I am all right! Tell me so directly, or, madam, I'll put you out of the window!"

I faltered out, " Oh, yes; you are perfectly well; nothing whatever is the matter with you. How could any one think other-wife?"

I fpoke in that way, having heard that infane people muft, for fafety's fake, be always humoured, whatever their vagrant fancies may be, and thank God I recollected the caution. The poor, deranged young man went on with his ravings.

"Ay! you are a fenfible young woman. You view the matter as every perfon fhould have done. But I might indeed have gone abfolutely mad; for, madam, they treated me like a dog—like an animal"—here he let go my wrift—"tied thofe two wrifts together—kept me in bed when nothing on earth ailed me. However, I had a fort of revenge, I bit the fheets to rags. And imagine a vile old wretch being placed in the room, who took away all my clothes—the horrid thief!—fed me with fpoon-meat, ay, and even my razors were nowhere to be found. But I determined to outwit their fuppofed clevernefs. Madam, I had a ftrange feeling. You know what that feeling is. Tell me inftantly you do; for I fee you have had fever yourfelf. You may have been even worfe than I was—perhaps really mad—infane—deranged—fay you have; ay, I fee you can enter into what my feelings were. Haven't you been mad?"— and he ftarted up, his eyes glaring more than before. I meekly anfwered, " Yes, fir, I know it all."

" Then you have been mad ? "—" Yes."

" There, now, I knew I was right; fo you fhall hear what I did. I had a wifh to put an end to myfelf. You muft know what that feeling is; you have alfo had the inclination; you have alfo feen a black imp in the corner of the room telling you how to do it ? Say you have—I know you have ! "—another tug at my poor wrift. So I gently faid, " Yes, I have feveral times wifhed to deftroy myfelf." " And feen the imp ? "— " Yes."— " Well, madam, and I fhould have done it, but for that vile beldame with her owliſh eyes always fixed on me. At laſt I feigned ſleep, and ſoon heard the old creature limping down ſtairs. Ha! what did I do? Sprang out of bed, ruſhed to the waſhſtand, ſmaſhed the drinking-glaſs, and ruſhed into bed again with two large pieces."

Here I thought it wiſe to pretend ignorance of his motive.

"What did you break the glaſs for?" ſaid I, my poor heart beating as faſt as before, yet I ſpoke in a quiet tone.

"What for? Why, you muſt know, madam, what my intention was. Something whiſpered in my ear—' Kill yourſelf, kill yourſelf.' You have heard that voice. I know you have—for you have evidently been worſe than I was—every feeling you have experienced. So, juſt on the point of working away at my throat, who ſhould bounce into the room but the lame creature, who was ſo inſpired, that ſhe really ruſhed at me, and,

Worſt.

with her iron grafp, forced me to relinquifh the glafs. 'Oh, my lad,' faid fhe, 'I 'll have none of them there pranks, fo pleafe to behave yourfelf, or there's a nice-fitting waiftcoat for you.' I believe I was a little ftrange, and no wonder, while enduring fuch treatment; but I have never had a return of fever from that time to this, and foon became as well as I am at this moment."

Then came another idiotic laugh, which frightened me almoft as much as his violence. After that he faid no more, leant back in the coach, apparently intent on the road, when, on coming in fight of a handfome houfe and grounds, he fprang up and called to the coachman, "Hallo, coachy! here I am at home; let me out, I fay." He was put down at the lodge-gate, and now that the paroxysm of infanity had paffed off, he refumed his former manner, and made me as elegant a bow as any nobleman might have done. Alas! poor young man! he was not fit to travel alone, although, on the prefent occafion, he might have got on quietly enough, if I had not unhappily hit on the tender word of his weakened brain—traveller. Indeed, his violence had fo unnerved me, it required all my kind friends' attention, on reaching High-ton Park, to calm my agitation. Lady B—— faid I fhould not again be fubjected to fuch a fcene of real danger; and that knife might have put it out of my power to be now writing this account of the tranfaction. There-fore, on returning to London, fhe fent her maid with me, and the journey was made without any awkward adventure.

Paft.

But this vifit was fated to be one of more intereft than I had anticipated.

Dear Maggie, before commencing thefe memoirs, I told you that mine was too un-eventful a life to note down its particulars; yet, as my pen runs on, and various fcenes arife from their hidden depths of memory, I begin to think the reverfe, and even while vifiting Highton Park a remarkable incident took place.

A lady, I fhould fay about thirty years of age, was ftaying in the houfe as a gueft, Lady B—— informed me, for fhe was uncomfortably fituated in life, her father, an influential country fquire, having taken a fecond wife, who infifted on Mifs Bingly feeking a home elfewhere. Having had an excellent education, fhe was well qualified to

Governefs. take a fituation as governefs, and Lady B—— mentioned her cafe to a friend who was intimate with a French lady, the fecond wife of an Italian nobleman, the Conte D'Orani. The Conte's daughter by the former marriage was about eighteen, and the Conteffa had one child, quite a young boy. While in England the Conteffa was inquiring for a lady to refide with her in Italy as governefs for their little fon, and alfo to be a friendly companion to herfelf, as fhe was much alone, the Conte generally being abfent, either in Florence or

Paris. The family refidence was quite in the country, an ifolated, gloomy, old caftle, and the Conteffa had fcarcely any fociety; but all this and other difcoveries Mifs Bingly made when, on accepting the fituation, fhe accompanied the Conteffa to Italy. She ftayed abroad about eighteen months, then returned to London and renewed the fociety of her former friends. She, however, was not communicative; far from it, for a kind of myftery feemed to hang over the caufe of her leaving fuch an eligible fituation: her lips feemed fealed on the fubject of what had taken place while fhe was in the caftle. All fhe faid was, that it was too dull a refidence to fuit her naturally lively difpofition, there being fo little fociety either vifiting at the caftle or in the neighbourhood, and alfo that the young Signorina Giulia was too overbearing and haughty to be under the control of any governefs. "In fact," faid Mifs Bingly, "after being there a month, I did not intend

Silence.

to ftay—I was much too unhappy—I could not remain for a continuance, although the Conteffa would have doubled my falary, and fhe was a charming perfon; but no power on earth fhould have kept me an hour after the time agreed on. I only regret I ftayed beyond the firft week."

In vain her friends demanded the caufe, but to no purpofe; fhe would reply to no queftions, always repeating, " I was too un-happy to ftay."

" Nor have I," faid Lady B——, while giving me thefe particulars, "the flighteft idea of her reafon, or why fhe is fo altered both in manner and appearance. She ufed to be lively and ever ready to oblige, now you muft perceive how grave and abftracted fhe is; there is evidently fomething on her mind which I have tried to get at,—not, I affure you, dear Mifs M'Donald, from idle curiofity, but from the wifh that fhe had a friend to confide in. We all know what a relief it

Solicitude.

is to an overburdened heart, to let it burſt the bonds of a concealed grief. Ah! little did Lady B—— know how my heart could reply to that ſentiment! " Beſides," continued her Ladyſhip, " Miſs Bingly is really not in ſpirits to take another ſituation, and as I have a ſincere regard for her, and pity her poſition, ſhe is moſt welcome to a home with me. I am not without the hope of ſome day ſo far thawing the ice of concealment as to induce her to tell me the cauſe of the extraordinary change that has come over her."

Sadness.

And little did Lady B—— then conceive that the ſtrange myſtery—at leaſt a part of it, for the after-details which I ſhall have to relate were moſt horrid—was to be explained on the following day.

Thus it was :——

We were ſitting in Lady B——'s morning-room, her Ladyſhip and I at needlework, Miſs Bingly as uſual with a book in hand, although too abſtracted to uſe it, nay, for matter of that, I verily believe ſhe held it upſide-down, when we were ſtartled by her uttering a violent ſcream. She ſprang from her ſeat, claſped her hands, and, with a horrified look, appeared to be addreſſing ſome one in the verandah. "O Giulia! Giulia! you wicked, bad girl! I thought as much! You have then killed her!" With thoſe words ſhe fell down in a ſwoon, nor was ſhe reſtored to her ſenſes for ſeveral hours. At laſt, on opening her eyes, ſhe ſighed deeply, and exclaimed, "Where am I? where is that dreadful girl? take her away!"

We gradually calmed her, and a flood of tears greatly relieved her, after which ſhe was able to tell us what had occaſioned the ſhock.

"I was in deep thought," ſaid ſhe, "my eyes fixed on the window, when the ſhadow of a female figure cloſely muffled up ſeemed to glide acroſs the verandah. She ſlowly raiſed the long veil, held out her hand, in which was a glafs goblet, and looked fixedly at me, with a triumphant yet ghaftly fmile; then turned the glafs as in the act of emptying it. Oh, horror! That phantom was Giulia d'Orani, and in her other hand was a bloody dagger!"

Poor Mifs Bingly was too agitated to fay more at that time, but later fhe fent for Lady B——, to whom fhe made the following difclofures.

"No doubt you have been furprifed, dear lady, by my fo conftantly refufing to ftate particulars relative to my manner of life while with the Conteffa in Italy, and the caufe of my leaving the caftle; and, indeed, up to yefterday I fhould ever have kept a ftrict filence on that painful fubject. But now it becomes needful I fhould break through that apparently ftrange filence, for from the appearance of that dreadful figure, I am led to believe that what I fo much feared has come to pafs. I feel certain the life of the amiable Conteffa has been taken away through the inftrumentality of her wicked ftep-daughter. Yes, Lady B——, you may well ftart. That bad girl hated the Conteffa, and even has gone fo far as to fay to me, that fhe would fome day filence her mifchievous tongue. Part of her hatred was caufed by the refufal of the Conte to fanction her marriage with a perfon of inferior birth and no fortune; and becaufe the Conteffa urged her to give up her lover, the wretched Giulia determined to feek an opportunity of wreaking vengeance for, as fhe faid, her ftep-mother's vile influence over her father.

Hate.

"I fufpected the manner fhe contemplated taking the poor lady's life, knowing the Signorina was not unacquainted with the nature of various poifons, which was the eafieft mode of effecting her purpofe, the Conteffa being in the habit of taking tifanes of many kinds; fo I carefully watched the girl's proceedings, and even had an antidote in cafe my poor friend's life fhould be attempted. For this reafon it was that I reluctantly agreed to ftay longer at the caftle; indeed, the Conteffa entreated me to do fo with tears; alfo the Conte faid he would be forry if I meditated leaving his little boy, who was fond of me, and paid attention to whatever I taught him. He was a very dear child, moft engaging; but altogether mine was an uncomfortable life, a daily witnefs of the Conteffa's unhappinefs, and having to endure the daughter's infolence. It was painful alfo to fee the Conte's indifference towards his wife, whom he had only married for her large fortune. They had but one fubject on which they could agree, and that was in thwarting the daughter's difgraceful love affair. But had I been even more unhappy, I could not in confcience have left the Conteffa at the mercy of fuch a bad-hearted girl, and might have remained, had not an attempt on my own life urged my departure. I fhall always think

The boy.

it was made in confequence of my having feen fome queer-looking fubftance in a bottle of medicine prepared for the Conteffa, my fufpicions being previoufly excited by Giulia's anxiety to afcertain whether the medicine had been taken. There was a thick fediment in the glafs, which the unfortunate lady was in the act of raifing to her lips! I rufhed acrofs the room, and dafhed away the glafs, juft in time to avert the cataftrophe. The Conteffa fhook her head, looking mournfully at me. I fee her now!—that laft look! 'Ah!' faid fhe, 'fome day—fome day!' That was all fhe uttered; but full well did I know fhe dreaded the fatal event. And now, dear Lady B——, it has happened, for the vifion I faw yefterday tells me fhe has died by foul play. Yes! and I have a ftrong prefentiment that the wicked young murderefs is alfo numbered with the dead. Alas! had I remained, the dear Conteffa might ftill be living. But how could I do fo? My life had been endangered by poiſoned ſoup. Yet, not knowing how to act, I conſulted an old lady who lived not far off: ſhe was Engliſh, a widow, and a great comfort to me in my lonelineſs. It was by her advice I determined to quit the hateful caſtle, though not without difficulty. The dear, amiable Conteſſa !—it coſt me much diſtreſs to part from her and her pretty boy. And it is the preſſure of a ſolemn promiſe ſhe exacted from me of not divulging the cauſe of my leaving that has kept me ſilent, and the conſtant dread of what might happen to her has taken away my energy and ſpirits. Do you forgive me, my dear friend ? for, indeed, I can ſcarce forgive myſelf for not having treated you with the confidence your kindneſs has ever merited."

Lady B—— begged ſhe would ſay no more, but be calm and compoſed, for which purpoſe ſhe was leaving the room, when Miſs Bingly called her back, with the requeſt that Miſs M'Donald might be made acquainted with what fhe termed "her melancholy tale." "I like that girl," fhe faid, "for fhe is fenfible, and muft be admired for her devotion to the Prince. Yes! I fhould wifh her to know why I have been fo dull, and unable to enjoy her agreeable fociety."

Egotift.

I am no egotift, Maggie, yet obliged to record thefe flattering remarks, or fhould be no true chronicler.

Mifs Bingly received a long letter, indeed, quite a packet, from her friend, Mrs Hutton, which arrived juft three days after the verandah-fcene. It had a black feal and the Italian poftmark, fo before it was opened we guefled the fatal contents. In truth, Mifs Bingly was too agitated to read it, and handed it to Lady B——. It was as follows,—for the hiftory of this unhappy family was fuch a curious one, fo full of painful romance, I requefted permiffion to take a copy, which I knew Lady Primrofe would feel interefted in perufing, and I infert it in thefe memoirs.

"Dear Miss Bingly,—I am truly diſtreſſed in ſending you ſad, very ſad news. Our dear Conteſſa is no more! and there is every appearance of her death having been cauſed by poiſon. Ah! our ſuſpicions were only too well founded, for that bad bold girl, in an exulting way, almoſt confeſſed the deed. But I muſt even ſhock you ſtill more, for the tragedy only two days ſince enacted in that odious caſtle will ſcarcely be credited. I feel at a loſs for words to expreſs how the horrid events occurred, and will try to be as conciſe as poſſible.

"*All three are gone—father, mother,* and *daughter!* I ſcarcely know what I am writing; but you will be ſo anxious for particulars. It ſeems the Conteſſa's confidential French maid was as ſtrict in guarding her miſtreſs againſt the plots of that wicked girl as you were; but poor Louiſe was lying dangerouſly ill, which, no doubt, gave the Signorina her long-wiſhed-for opportunity.

Murder.

The poison was administered in a glass of Hungary water,—the doctor says so openly; but not all his skill could save her. The Conte, I must say, is very kind, and declares the perpetrator shall be brought to justice, even should the assassin be his own daughter; but he will not believe her guilty. His brother-in-law is at the castle,—Monsieur de St Marlean,—and he attended the funeral with other relations of the Contessa, who left immediately afterwards. Monsieur is going to have the affair thoroughly investigated; even if it should be necessary to exhume the body. *The daughter's hand destroyed her father!* The details are frightful. She had a violent altercation with the Conte, in such a loud tone as to be overheard from the apartment adjoining his study. She braved his authority, saying, she was resolved on marrying that low man—you know whom I mean —and demanded as a right the money falling to her share on the Contessa's death.

Horror.

" ' Never,' faid the Conte, ' fhall you inherit a fous of your victim's property ! ' "

" ' Victim ! ' fhe cried, in a fcoffing tone; Shame. ' prove your words, my Lord! Ay! if you dare to defy me, or refufe to fign thefe papers which are duly prepared by a notary, giving me on your death full poffeffion of the caftle and eftates, I will damage your reputation in fuch a way you will be obliged to fly this country, and perhaps hide in your dear favourite France, from which hated clime you thought it fit to bring a woman to place as a ftep-mother over my head. But enough of that ftory, all now finifhed. Sign thofe papers, or I will be avenged.'

" ' Giulia ! ' fighed the poor father, ' you have ever been a moft undutiful heartlefs daughter. I cannot control your difgraceful marriage intentions, but thefe eftates are hereditary and '——

" ' I know they are, and I am your eldeft born.'

"'Not fo; they will belong to my fon.'

"'Oh! then you wifh to place that puny brat over my head!' She gave an ironical fmile. 'But my dear little brother requires a fifter's care and attention—he muft have medicine—a *ftrong dofe,* my Lord!'

"'Giulia! wicked girl! you muft be mad to entertain fuch horrid ideas! Surely one victim will fuffice on whom to work your wickednefs!'

"'Say thefe words again at your peril, and I will—— but ftay; fign thofe papers,' fhe cried out, with a menacing attitude, 'or dread my vengeance!'

"'Never! I will not fign away my boy's inheritance!'

Struggle. "After thefe words fcuffling founds were heard, and a deep groan, mingling with dreadful fhrieks.

"The attendants rufhed in. Oh, what a horrid fight! There lay the Conte almoft dying from a dagger-wound in the breaft, and the wretched Giulia extended on the floor in a pool of blood—dead! The point of a dagger was ſtill in her heart. The table was overturned, ſo the ſuppoſition is, that in the act of ſtabbing her father, ſhe had dragged the table over her, in the fall occaſioning another unſheathed dagger to ſtrike her wicked heart. No doubt it all occurred in this way, for ſhe was of too cowardly a nature to attempt her own life, therefore the crime of ſelf-murder is fortunately not to be added to her black catalogue of crime! The ſheath of the dagger was in her girdle.

Nemeſis.

" The Conte ſurvived only an hour; gaſping for breath, he was unable to ſpeak beyond a few almoſt indiſtinct words to Monſieur de St Marlean, in whoſe hand he placed thoſe of the poor orphaned child. His look was ſupplicating. Monſieur underſtood his meaning. 'Yes, D'Orani,' ſaid he, 'I accept the charge, and will never forſake my nephew.'

" The Conte faintly ſmiled, his eyes became

fixed and glaſſy, and with a deep groan he expired.

" He will be interred with the Conteſſa in the family-vault. Alas! ſo ſoon to be re-opened. Not ſo the young murdereſs! for the neighbours are ſo exaſperated, eſpecially the peaſantry, that ſome of them declare they will kick the coffin to pieces, and throw the body in a deep pit! therefore ſhe is to be buried at an unknown hour, perhaps at night. Thus ends this dreadful affair. I feel quite upſet at witneſſing ſuch horrors!

" You remember Madame de St Marlean—a nice perſon! Monſieur inquired for you, re-gretting you were no longer with little Henri. It is melancholy to hear the poor child; he is ſo conſtantly lamenting his 'petite maman.' I really think, if you would like to be ſo placed, they would be very glad for you to reſide with them near Paris, and to have the ſuperintendence of the little boy. In faɛt, Monſieur told me to hint the ſubjeɛt to you;

ſo think of it, dear Miſs Bingly, and give an anſwer ſoon.

"I cannot write any more. It will be ſome time before I ſhall get over the events of the laſt few days. Write ſoon to

"Your ſincere friend,

JANE HATTON."

This ſad hiſtory made us all melancholy, and poor Miſs Bingly was quite overcome. She reflected on her friend's advice, and accepted Sir Archibald's kind offer of communicating with Monſieur de St Marlean; ſo, when I left my kind friends to return to Lady Primroſe, to whoſe houſe Sir Archibald kindly eſcorted me, on taking leave of Miſs Bingly, ſhe told me that it was her intention to travel almoſt immediately to France, and take charge of her little favourite.

But I leave this melancholy tale, and go on to ſay how tired I ſoon became of the conſtant whirl of London faſhionable life—out

Sympathy.

all day in her Ladyſhip's coach, and every night
to ſome public place : different kinds of amuſement to while away the late hours. I was
ſick of the compliments paid me ; indeed,
in many caſes the attentions of gentlemen
went beyond compliments. I am fearful of
being thought vain in repeating ſuch matters, yet, after the lapſe of ſo many years,
I may ſay, that, had I been ſo diſpoſed, I
might have been moſt eligibly married, for I
had offers far above me in poſition and wealth.
The eldeſt ſon of a Cambrian baronet, well
known for his riches and the poſſeſſion of a
noble eſtate, was very devoted; he really
ſeemed attached to me, and his ſuit was
warmly advocated by his friend, Lady Primroſe ; yet it pained me to rejeᾶ a perſon evidently amiable and talented. I could not
acknowledge the reſidence of a partiality
in my heart for one who had perhaps
forgotten me. So, Maggie, the beaux who
flattered a ſimple Highland laſſie with propo-

sals of marriage, could not succeed in their hopes. But enough of this.

It was reported to me that the Princess of Wales had been displeased by Lady Margaret M'Donald having appeared at court (she was obliged to go, Sir Alexander having been in attendance on the hateful Duke of C——), saying, " She was sorry she had not previously known that Lady Margaret had been concerned in the escape of the Pretender."

" Well, madam," replied Prince Frederick, to whom the remark was made, " suppose you had known it! Would you not have acted in the same manner if that unfortunate man had appeared before you in such calamitous circumstances ? I know, I am sure, you would."

Rebuke.

No doubt the Princess felt the rebuke, and was ashamed of such a heartless speech.

Regarding myself, I heard the Prince would not allow any one to speak but with becoming respect relative to Prince

Charles's escape. He once said, " he could appreciate the worth of my exertions, although they were used for the safety of a rival."

Prince Frederick was an amiable man, noble minded and generous in character, far different to his father, who was passionate, obstinate, and dreadfully stingy in his habits. Therefore, the father and son being so opposite in disposition, the reports bruited about of their disagreements occasioned no surprise to those who could withdraw the veil from the concealment of inner court-life.

And one day I saw passing in a royal coach such a pretty child—Prince George, the son of Prince Frederick—who, many years from this time, mounted the throne, the property of the Stuarts, as George III. of Great Britain; for Prince Frederick dying in 1751, this boy, then only thirteen years of age, succeeded his grandfather, Old Geordie, as he was always named in the Highlands.

I was returned to Skye when Prince Frederick died, and truly concerned I was to hear of the ſad event. But how I do digreſs! My friends will be tired of reading all this. So I go on to the time of my leaving the hoſpitable roof of dear Lady Primroſe; for, after receiving the Government pardon, oh! how I longed to be at home again. Alſo, I was tired of being ſtared at; for ſuch an ado was made of the little act by which the dear Prince had eſcaped, as never was the like! The curioſity of the people was really annoying. Sometimes I felt the colour mount to my cheeks, and tears in my eyes, when young men ſo far forgot what was due, not only to a ſtranger in their country, but to the ſhrinking timidity of a ſimple-minded girl, as to ſtand in groups around the doors of the houſes where I accompanied Lady Primroſe to parties and routs to look at me! And frequently I heard diſloyal remarks about Prince Charles, which vexed me

Vexed.

even more than their inconsiderate rudeness to myself.

Return.

But all this was to come to an end, for the time drew nigh for me to begin journeying to dear Scotland. The recollection of its blue hills and sweet heather was too deeply impressed on my memory to make me regret quitting England; nor could I ever wish to revisit a land where so many of my days had been passed in anxiety and weariness. Nay, even while my kind hostess did all she could to amuse and cheer me up, yet the uneasiness I was enduring about all the dear people at home, no one had a distant idea of. I think her Ladyship guessed my secret wish to be with those I loved; for one day, while at our needle, she remarked on my altered looks, which she supposed was caused by the close air and late hours of London life. "So, my dear, although I wish you could stay with me altogether, yet, as health is the first consideration, and much I shall grieve to part with you, my dear creature, I muft not be felfifh; your friends muft be wearying for your return. Only you muft not think of going until I fhall have arranged a nice plan for your travelling comfortably home. What do you think of Malcolm M'Leod being at liberty, and about to return to Raafay? I heard this yefterday. So, my dear, it is all fettled in this head of mine, that you and he, and that half-mad fcarecrow Katie, fhall journey back together—the opportunity is too good to be loft. And another thing I have to tell you. Now, my dear, your Highland pride muft not be offended by the knowledge of my having raifed a little fortune for the fair ' Prince's Preferver.' Ay! my dear,—do not look fo aftonifhed,—I have been about it all this time. And now look here, my dear foul! here 's a nice prefent to take back to your home."

She went to a cabinet, and drew out an

Efcort.

Dowry.

elegantly-knitted filk purfe, faying, as fhe placed it in my band, "There's juft fifteen hundred pounds—a pretty little fum," added fhe, fignificantly, "to help on the intended wedding." Then fhe kiffed me and fmiled. I knew the allufion, for Lady Primrofe had often joked me about having an admirer in a fly corner, on occafions when I declined receiving attentions from one gentleman in particular whom fhe much wifhed me to marry. I fear at this moment my confcious cheeks told her the true tale. "Well, my dear, there's no controlling thefe little heart affections. Be married and happy, dear Flora! and may I live to fee you fo, fhould I ever vifit again the bonnieft of all countries—my native Scotland.

Was fhe not kind, this dear lady, who had been like a fecond mother during all my troubles?

Well, true to her word, the very next day Malcolm M'Leod came to dinner; and well do I remember how he made us laugh by mentioning a circumſtance which happened while the Prince was concealed in a cave during his wanderings in Raaſay. "Only two men were with him," ſaid Malcolm. "I forget their names,—a M'Donald, of courſe, Miſs Flora"—looking archly at me—"for Charlie always managed to have one of that faithful clan with him."

On this occaſion they were foraging for proviſions, and left the Prince alone. Night came on, and having no light, he lay down in his plaid, and tried not to feel the hard rough ſtones under him; but the intenſe cold drove away all chance of ſleep. Then recollecting an old blanket which was in a bundle at the end of this diſmal hole, he ſprang up, groping his way down the cave, which was ſo narrow, that by ſtretching out his arms he could touch the ſides. It was a gradual deſcent towards the end, not more than three feet in height.

Content.

As he advanced thus flowly, he heard a queer found, like the clattering of a perfon's teeth from cold. Naturally thinking of a concealed enemy, and having not even a ftick to defend himfelf, he thought of retreating, when, through the chinks of the broken rock—his eyes by this time more accuftomed to the gloom—a ftrange fight made him ftart.

"And what d'ye think it was? My lady, ye'll never guefs. I can't help laughing when I tell this ftory, and fo did his Royal

Highnefs afterwards. A poor little old monkey, fitting all of a heap, fhivering and clattering his jaws like a pair of nut-crackers!" But the wife creature had tried to make himfelf comfortable under exifting circumftances, having burft open the bundle, fcattered the things about, ftuck a red nightcap on his head in moft jaunty fafhion, and wrapt around him was the blanket intended to fhelter the fhoulders of royalty! Oh! he grinned and chattered, with fuch ftrange howlings, the Prince feared the noife would attract the attention of the fentinels who were everywhere about.

However, the fage gentleman clung to his ftolen property, refifting every attempt of the rightful owner to gain poffeffion of the blanket.

Fancy the furprife of the two men when they returned, and faw their Prince fide by fide with fuch a companion! The poor animal had probably entered the cave for fhelter, and was nearly dead from hunger; but after having had the honour of partaking of food with the Prince, in due time it received a hint to leave, being driven forcibly from the cave. The Prince ufed to enjoy this joke, and in mentioning it always imitated the animal's queer geftures. He fuppofed it had efcaped from fome private refidence in the neighbourhood, as monkeys were fo feldom feen in thofe parts; and during their three days' hiding they never faw any more

A pair.

of their ſavage friend. "Perhaps," added
Malcolm, "the fare was not good enough
for the gentleman, being only dry cheeſe
and oatmeal, with nothing but water from
a ſpring hard by. Poor Charlie! how he
would have done juſtice to a dinner like this,
my Lady Primroſe!"

"Ay! and I wiſh his Royal Highneſs was
here to partake of it; indeed, how happy I
ſhould be to know where he is at this
moment. But I will not deſpair of ſeeing
him ſome day, when Charlie ſhall come 'to
tak' his ain again.'" This line her Ladyſhip
was ſo fond of repeating, from a ſong of the
day! And, dear Maggie, I have good reaſons
for believing that Lady Primroſe did not only
ſee Prince Charles, but received him into her
houſe for a few days, when he was in London
many years after under a diſguiſed name.
The reaſon was obvious, although no other
attempt has ever been made of his "takin'
his ain again."

And now all was fettled for our journey two days after. Her Ladyfhip managed every-thing—hired a conveyance—helped me and Katie with our packing, not forgetting to flip in the boxes fundry ufeful articles as remem-brances—and infifting on being at all the expenfe of the journey. As for my kind-hearted companion, he was vaftly amufed when told he was to take charge of me.

" Why, Mifs Flora ! " faid Malcolm, " here am I, who came up to London to be hanged, going back to Scotland in grand ftyle, and with you in a braw poft-chaife ! "

He congratulated me on my little fortune, but its poffeffion did not make me feel com-fortable ; the fact of a fubfcription rather annoyed me, and poffibly would be difpleafing to my Highland relations. However, to have refufed the money would have juftly offended my excellent patronefs ; fo the long purfe was carefully enfconced at the bottom of the travelling-trunk.

Pride.

Nor muſt I forget to mention a lovely gift Lady Primroſe made me, by placing on my finger ſuch an elegant ring which, ſhe ſaid, I was never to wear without remembering her.

The ring.

I think, Maggie, you have ſeen it. However, for my other friends who may read theſe jottings of a deſultory pen, I will deſcribe it. In a baſket of the fineſt gold filigree was contained a tiny bunch of wee roſes compoſed of diamonds and leaves of green enamel and emeralds; the part round the finger was a band of white enamel, with an inſcription in ſmall gilded letters, in Latin, the meaning of which was, " Flora, Preſerver of the White Roſe ! " Oh, ſo pretty ! I had many more articles of jewellery given me by various ladies, who were ſo kind as to ſay they never could do enough for me; but this beautiful ring I preferred to all the other preſents, and I knew it would pleaſe every one at home, the device being ſo gracefully complimentary.

Well, after nearly finifhing our travelling arrangements, tired enough I was, for Lady Primrofe infifted on taking me to call on fuch a number of people who were anxious to bid good-bye to Flora M'Donald; fo I felt quite overwhelmed when, the chaife at the door, Malcolm in readinefs as the efcort, and honeft Katie waiting for me to ftep in after having arranged the parcels to her liking, I threw my arms around the dear miftrefs of the houfe, who had fo befriended me. We were both in tears. In another moment the fteps of the chaife were pufhed back, the door banged to, the poftboy cracked his whip, and off we were!

Parting.

I cannot defcribe my fenfations, mingled as they were with joy at going home, and regret at leaving fome dear friends, whom it was not likely I fhould again meet.

I promifed to write occafionally to Lady Primrofe, and did fo, until her death a few years fince.

While we journeyed on, Malcolm told me of much that had paſſed in the Highlands during the laſt few months relative to the Prince's movements, he having conduȼted his Royal Highneſs from Raaſay to many other places,—to the M'Donalds of Morar, the M'Donalds of Borrodale and Glenaladale, and the M'Kinnons of Corry. John M'Kinnon was Malcolm's brother-in-law, and he took a warm intereſt in the royal fugitive, and during ſome of their wanderings the Prince was diſguiſed as his ſervant, paſſing by the name of Lewis Caw, the ſuppoſed ſon of a ſurgeon in Crieff.

Diſguiſe.

Malcolm related an amuſing tale of the Prince while going about as his ſervant. In the courſe of their wanderings, they had fallen into a bog, ſo, on reaching the houſe of John M'Kinnon at Ellagol, the Captain told the girl in Gaelic to bring hot water and waſh his feet. While ſhe was doing this, he ſaid, pointing to the poor, deſpiſed, ill-looking Lewis

Caw, "You fee that poor fellow yonder? How fick he is! It will be a charity to clean his feet. Indeed, he more needs attending to than I do."

"What!" faid fhe, "afk me to do fuch a fervice? No; if I wafh the feet of your father's fon, they are the mafter's; but to touch the toes of his mother's fon—a low peafant! very fine truly! No; I canna do it!"

Malcolm, however, at laft perfuaded the offended damfel to lower her dignity; but, in the act of wafhing poor Charles's legs and feet, fhe was fo crofs at being obliged to do it, fo very rough in her handling, he begged M'Leod to defire her not to rub fo hard. He fpoke low, left fhe fhould hear he had no Gaelic.

"And truly a ftrange figure he was," faid Malcolm; "his wig taken off, an old clout of a handkerchief on his head, with a cotton nightcap drawn over it, and leather thongs inftead of buckles to his old brogues; fuch a

Servant-
galifm.

guy! his own mother wouldn't have found him out!"

Old Corry had accompanied them, and would have gone farther, but the Prince declined his fervices in confequence of his age; fo John M'Kinnon of Ellagol continued his guide until his Highnefs was left in Borrodale's charge; and M'Kinnon, on returning homewards, had nearly reached his houfe when he was taken by a party of militia, fent up to London, where, after fome months' imprifonment, he was allowed to go back to Scotland. "In truth, Mifs Flora," faid Malcolm, "we are all lucky to efcape fo well; but I fuppofe that wretched Duke of C—— has hanged fo many, he is tired of fuch fun. Thefe miffortunes have deeply affected our unhappy Prince. I often heard him murmuring in his broken fleep, fpeaking incoherently in Italian, French, and Englifh. Once he faid diftinctly, 'O God! poor Scotland!' It fair grieved me, for it fhowed how bitter his thoughts were."

Captain M'Leod alfo told me of a curious fact connected with his Royal Highnefs's hairbreadth efcape—a fingular circumftance.

When hard preffed in the direction of Glenmorrifton, he was indebted to a band of feven Highlanders for protection during feveral days. Thefe men, having fought for their Prince, could be trufted. They were felf-outlawed, to fave their lives from a cruel Government, fupporting themfelves as beft they could; and bad enough as that was, the fituation of their unfortunate Prince was a great deal worfe, he having been obliged to take fhelter from the mufket-fhots of the foldiery, who were fcouring the country to deftroy the poor creatures who had fled in terror to hide themfelves amongft the hills. The Prince had never been in greater danger, fo the party of faithful M'Donalds then conducting him hurriedly concealed him in a fmall hole amongft the bufhes. Alas! how miferable muft have been this place! fo narrow and fhort, that he

Friends.

could not lie at full length, and expofed to hunger, fatigue, and rain in torrents.

In this diftrefs the party refolved to have recourfe to " the feven men of Glenmorrifton," as they were called, knowing they were to be found fomewhere in that neighbourhood.

Their names were Gregor, Alexander, Donald, and Hugh, of the Chifholm clan, John and Alexander M'Donald, and Patrick Grant. At firft, the rank of the Prince was concealed from them, but on going to the place of meeting, they recognifed him, fo the three prefent took an oath of fidelity to their royal mafter. The others, who were at a diftance foraging for plunder, returned the

Oaths. next day, and they alfo fwore to be faithful; indeed, fo truly did they keep their pledge, that not until they heard, long after, of the Prince's fafe arrival in France, did they ac- knowledge having affifted him.

With thefe rough yet good-hearted men he was kept for three weeks, well fed, and at night made as comfortable as a bed of freſh heather admitted of, and one of them was often ſent to Fort Auguſtus for information reſpecting the Prince's chance of getting away to France. "And what do you think," ſaid Malcolm, "of a noble gift to the Prince from one of the band, on returning from Fort Auguſtus? You 'll never gueſs, Miſs Flora, ſo I 'll juſt tell you. It was a pennyworth of gingerbread! which the poor fellow thought would be conſidered a dainty bit for his Royal Highneſs.

A gift.

We both enjoyed this joke, which I only mention as a proof of the man's kind feeling. They accompanied the Prince and his companions as far as Loch Arkaig, and then, after a friendly farewell, returned to their wild courſe of life.

And now, Maggie, I will tell you a curious ſtory I heard many years ago about one of theſe men, Hugh Chiſholm, who, when in Edinburgh, was viſited by ſeveral perſons from whom he received fums of money, but in fhaking hands he always gave his left, faying, that "as his right hand had been fhaken by the Prince at parting, from that moment he refolved never to give his right hand to any man until he faw Charles Stuart again." A ftrange fancy was it not? I wonder whether he was more courteous to ladies!

I alfo heard that when the Prince got fafely acrofs the water, he fent thefe men

Reward.

twenty-four guineas, as a recompenfe for their rude hofpitality at a time when he was forely in need of help.

It was about this period that poor young Roderick M'Kenzie met his death. He had ferved in the Prince's regiment of life-guards, and being tall and elegant-looking, alfo fome-what refembling him in countenance, he might well have been miftaken for his Royal Highnefs. While fkulking in the Braes of Glenmorrifton he encountered a body of Hanoverian foldiers, and attempted to efcape, but they furrounded him; fo knowing his life muft be forfeited, and recollecting his likenefs to the Prince, he exclaimed, in a tone of authority, "Villains! you have flain your Prince."

A loyal lie.

The foldiers, delighted at having fecured their prize, cut off the head of the unfortunate young man, took it to Invernefs, and there are people who fay that the brutal Duke of C—— had it packed in a bafket, and journeyed with the ghaftly treafure to London. However, on its being fhown to one Morifon, a former valet of the Prince, who nearly fainted at the horrid fight, he fwore pofitively it was not the head of his royal mafter. Poor M'Kenzie! his fate was hard, and let us hope he was pardoned for dying with an untruth on his lips.

But to continue our journey.

On reaching York, we went by invitation to the houfe of Dr Burton. This gentleman had juft been liberated from a long confinement in jail for the part he took in ferving the Prince.

We were not there many days, for I was fo impatient to get home to my dear mother, and feel fecured in our quiet retreat from future danger. The troubles I had undergone were beginning to affect my health, but all was forgotten, and my heart cheered, when the firft peep of the blue hills reached my eager fight. The "Highland rofe" was not fo bright as formerly, yet it would now foon regain its hue and vigour.

Home.

But let me pafs over the happy meeting with my mother and kind ftep-father, who could now praife me for what I had done, which commendation added to the pride I felt in exhibiting all the prefents given to me from fo many grand people,—"to be kept," faid Armadale, "as heir-looms in the family." And fo they are, dear Maggie, as you fo well know, having feen fo many of the pretty articles which ornament our beft room; and I have alfo

ſome trinkets of value, that I wear on grand·
occaſions.

When I came to the bottom of the box,   *The purſe.*
and in a heſitating way placed the purſe
in my ſtep-father's hand, telling him its
hiſtory, he remarked, "The money being
given you in kindneſs, it muſt be accepted as
ſuch; yet I would rather it had not been
offered."

I aſſured him, that was alſo my feeling,
but dear Lady Primroſe would not hear
of a refuſal, which alone induced me to take
it.

Malcolm M'Leod was preſent when this
was ſaid, and came to my reſcue.

"Indeed, Miſs Flora, ye could not do leſs
than accept the bounty, for otherwiſe the good
leddy would have gone right demented. Ye
weel deſerved the filler, and more than as
much again."

The kind-hearted Malcolm ſaid this on
parting, ſhaking me warmly by the hand as

he left us, after a few days' ftay at Armadale, to return to Raafay.

So, when I was comfortably fettled at home, again taking to my quiet occupations, after feeing thofe of my friends in the neighbourhood who were curious to learn all the adventures which had befallen "The Prince's Preferver;" the joy of meeting dear Angus, who came over from Miltoun to welcome back his "rebel" fifter, as he jokingly termed me; the pleafure of renewing our country walks, rides, and unchaining the wee boatie for a fail on the friendly lake; my little pony neighing and rubbing its rough head on my fhoulder, while honeft Sidger, jealous of any attention to another favourite, barked and gambolled around his happy miftrefs to his heart's content;—all this brought me my former peace of mind. I will now confefs why I had named him Sidger: it reminded me of one then far away, a *foldier* with his regiment, for that is the meaning of the Gaelic word.

Old faces.

Every day I gleaned fome news of the changes which had occurred during the many months I had been abfent, and amongft them none pained me more than hearing of the unhappinefs of our dear friends at Rowan's Dyke, the M'Dougals, who were made fo miferable by the lofs of their fon, my former tormenting admirer, poor half-mad Jamie.

It feems that after ferving as mate of a merchant fhip, the veffel was wrecked off the coaft of Guinea, and all the crew fuppofed to have perifhed, for none were ever heard of, except our poor lad, who was wafhed afhore, nearly dead from exhauftion and hunger. He had been for two days on a fmall rock in the ocean, expofed to the rays of a burning fun, which at laft was fo overpowering, he muft have loft all confcioufnefs, and been dafhed by the waves off the rock, more dead than alive. In this wretched ftate he was found by a moft excellent man, who took him to his houfe. He was a Romifh prieft, who

Caftaway.

Oafis.

had lived for years in that defolate fpot with a favourite nephew, whofe recent death had nearly broken the old man's heart. He was fo loved and refpected by the few inhabitants of that quite remote part of the world, they fought his advice in all their little affairs, and many a poor foul was he the means of comforting in their earthly diftreffes, and pointing them to the path of everlafting peace and joy. Although a foreigner, yet he had a flight knowledge of Englifh, by which means he made out poor Jamie's hiftory as foon as his weakened ftrength enabled him to fpeak, but it was many days before he gave a fign of recollection. The poor people were fo kind in their humble way, and the good father watched him with the anxiety of a parent.

"Dear boy," faid the worthy man, " God has taken my laft fupport, the prop of my old age; therefore, fhould it be His bleffed will to reftore you, ftay with me, be in his place, the comfort and folace of my old

age. I will leave you all I poſſeſs, and
when ſummoned to a brighter world, you
can return to your native land. It will not
be for long; I feel the aged tree is bending
beneath the blaſt it has lately endured."

But it was nǫt ſo to be. The poor lad
rallied for a few days, and then gradually
ſank; the ſhock had been too much for
a frame previouſly weakened by the heavy
drudgery of a ſeafaring life. And when
all was over, the good prieſt mourned his
loſs, and buried him by the rites of the
Romiſh Church, in the ſame grave with his
nephew.

Poor
Jamie!

All theſe particulars were ſent to the
family at Rowan's Dyke as ſoon as the old
man had the opportunity of meeting with a
perſon who could write a clear letter in Engliſh,
which was not for ſome months, and he
alſo managed to ſend home the remains of
poor Jamie's ſilver watch. I ſay the remains,
for with the knocking about on the rocks,

it was broken in pieces, the works and cafe fmafhed almoft flat. However, fuch as it was, the unhappy parents have treafured it as a melancholy remembrance of their haplefs boy. The old laird was almoft befide himfelf with grief, nor lefs bitter were the mother's feelings, although in a great meafure confoled by the information that Jamie had expreffed on his death-bed fincere

Repents. contrition for having caufed his parents 10 much forrow, and had he lived, he would have returned to them a changed chara&er. Alas! poor fellow! there certainly had been room for improvement.

My early friend Jeffie M'Dougal was well married during my abfence, but as her home is in a diftant ifland, it is not likely we fhall often meet. She has no family. It is now many years fince the old man died; he never recovered the lofs of his idolifed fon; and Mrs M'Dougal lived to a great age, refpe&ed and loved by all in the neighbourhood, by none more fo than myfelf, although there was fuch a difference in age. Rowan's Dyke is ftill ftanding, but poffeffed by other parties.

How true is the remark of fome author, that in this world, if we feek for more happi-nefs than can be afforded by a feeling of calm contentment, we muft expect to reap difap-pointment ! In my heart's core there was a fpot filled with anxiety, nor was it removed for many weeks after returning home, until the joyful news, which had been long in coming, reached our diftant part of the world, that the dear Prince was fafely landed on the coaft of Bretagne, and was to proceed from *France.* Morlaix to Paris.

I think I have before mentioned that Niel M'Eachan had accompanied his royal mafter, and a letter came from that worthy man, giving moft interefting particulars of their hairbreadth efcape from danger, the veffel having been chafed by two Britifh fhips of war. Alas! poor Prince! he had to encounter peril even at the laſt moment of leaving his dear Scotland.

Niel ſaid the Prince deſpatched two letters from Morlaix, one to his father, King James, and a ſecond to his brother, Prince Henry.

Later, we heard of Prince Charles being well received at the French Court; but after a while, it ſeems, he gave offence to King Louis, and was ordered to quit Paris. Then he went to Avignon, from which town M'Eachan's laſt letter for ſome years was dated. No doubt, he wrote ſometimes, but at that period it was difficult to get letters from foreign parts, and a news-gazette was an event to the family who received it, obliging them to make it a circulating epiſtle for weeks afterwards. In theſe days, matters have altered for the better, for although, like angels' viſits, "few and far between," yet we are occaſionally gratified in our quiet nook with the ſight of a news-ſheet.

Knowing of the Prince's fafety relieved my mind; my fervices and troubles in his caufe had not been in vain : this certainly was a fatiffaction which drew out one thorn from its concealed recefs in my heart.

And now, dear Maggie, as I write this narrative to intereft you, I will relate a circumftance that occurred in our family about this time, caufing fome talk amongft the neighbours. It will amufe you, Maggie, and I cannot help fmiling while writing it down.

My half-fifter Annabella had grown from a fine girl into a handfome young woman, and was generally admired by thofe who had an opportunity of fearching out fuch a violet in the fhade. | A beauty.

One day a gentleman, who was faid to be ftaying in the village, occupying the only ftranger's room the little inn afforded, came to Armadale Houfe, fent in his name-card, requefting to be favoured by feeing " The Prince's Preferver." Now this I knew full

Smitten.

well was but the pretext for a call, as we had noticed him the Sabbath before, making ufe of his eyes in Annabella's direction, which had rather difconcerted the poor girl; therefore, on his now prefenting himfelf at our houfe, my mother and I—for my father and Angus were out—received him very coldly.

However he talked away, telling us about himfelf; that he was Englifh, a baronet's fon, unmarried, very fond of fcientific purfuits, in fact it was a geologifing expedition which had brought him to the Highlands, and that hearing of Mifs Flora M'Donald's fame, he was defirous not only to fee that celebrated young lady, but alfo to make her acquaintance, and that of her amiable family.

While he rambled on in this flattering ftrain, I had time to recollect having heard the name on his card during my long ftay in London. It was a good name, but I refrain from mentioning it, he having returned to his eftate, 1 fuppofe, and the object of his affections, my dear fifter, being now married and comfortably fettled at Cuidrach, furrounded by a group of pretty young things. So I will call him Mr Smith, as being lefs likely to be traced, that name being, I am told, the moft numerous in England. Well, now to defcribe him. He was very plain, I thought ugly, and by no means gentlemanly in appearance; nearly forty, with dark hair and whifkers, fhort, and rather ftout.

Such was Annabella's admirer, for fo he proved to be after a few weeks' acquaintance; and whether walking, riding, or boating, join us he would, fo we were forced to fubmit. Once in the houfe, he was fcarcely ever away from it. I never faw a man more in love, but to no avail, for my fifter hated him. At laft our father was obliged to tell him to dif-continue attentions which were really annoy-ing. Befides, he was too fond of his glafs, for in addition to ufing a fmall hammer for knock-ing about all the rocks and hills in the country

Looks.

in fearch of wondrous fpecimens, he alfo, report faid, was given to ftrike off the heads of fundry bottles of brandy, which well accounted for his face being fo coarfe and red. He gave one the idea of being, if not abfolutely tipfy, rarely quite fober. Horrid man ! a fine beau for my darling, fweet-mannered fifter.

Hated.

As for Angus, he could not tolerate a perfon who, although a gentleman, did not conduct himfelf as one. And rich too, he was ; I cannot tell the liberal fettlements my fifter would have had.

But now comes the comic part of the ftory, which you will like to hear, Maggie ; for I know you are a merry girl, who enjoys a little fun.

Well, this Mr Smith could not tear himfelf from the village, although a hopelefs lover ; and at laft became fo troublefome, that my father forbade his coming to Armadale, fo we faw nothing of him for perhaps a month, when one night, juſt after ſupper, we were preparing for our uſual Scripture-reading, when a loud knocking at the outer ſhutters and front door alarmed us; we thought a thief was trying to enter. My ſtep-father and Angus ruſhed to the entrance, when who ſhould have cauſed the diſturbance, but our worry and torment, old Smith, and ſo intoxicated, that the gentle- men called to us to run up the ſtair out of his way ! However, we heard his vulgar voice, as all in the houſe muſt have done, bawling out how he loved his own dear Annabella, and would not be denied an entrance by all the lawyers or conſtables of the land; a ſingle lock of his loved one's hair he would have— ay! that very night too; and to obtain it he would fight his way even by fire and faggot !

The man did not know what he was ſaying, nor could he be pacified. Armadale tried to coax him away, but all attempts were vain. As for my brother, he was ſo irritated, we

Drunk.

thought the men would have come to blows; for although out of the way, yet from the upper-landing we faw all that paffed. Suddenly, to our aftonifhment, Angus burft out laughing: a ftrange thought came into his head. "Stay; father let him alone: he fhall have a lock of hair; for the drunken fellow will not go away without it." So faying, he mounted the ftair, laughing immoderately.

"O Angus! what have you faid? how could you make fuch a promife? he fhall not have it!"

I faid this rather angrily, feeling annoyed.

The pony.

"Tut! tut! you filly girl! It's only fome of the pony's mane he fhall have. Why the man is fo drunk, he'll not know the difference; fo quick, give me the fciffors, and find a piece of bright ribbon to tie it up! Our Annabella's hair muft be prefented in due form and with becoming refpect. Do make hafte, it will be rare fun!" He rufhed off, and, I am fure, was not away five minutes, came up-ftairs, met us with a lovely bit of fky-blue ribbon, to tie up the precious lock of my pony's fhock head in moft approved fafhion.

We eagerly waited the conclufion of the pantomime, all our alarm having changed to merriment, which was fhared by my father alfo on knowing the caufe.

Mr Smith was ftill violent, but when Angus went towards him with the neat little packet, faying, as he held it firmly in his hand, "There, Sir, is the prize you wifh for. With much difficulty I have fucceeded in obtaining it: even a kick from the young lady I have had to encounter; for believe me, the owner of that hair is at times a troublefome, high-mettled, fpirited fair one. Treafure the gift, and I hope you will duly value it, and efti-mate the compliment paid you, for never before has any gentleman received a love-lock from your adored one's head—on my honour, this is the firft ever taken from it."

All this time the man was ftaring and

Treafure.

Satyr.

blinking his ftupid eyes, feemingly not to comprehend my brother's meaning, until a fnatch at the paper revealed the coveted hair, and then his geftures and antics would have fuited the rare exhibition I faw in London of a clown's performance; for he fkipped with delight, kiffed it, and placing it near his heart, vowed that Angus was a right good jolly boy, whom he fhould love as a brother; never, no never more, fhould he and his dear Annabella be parted.

Oh! it was fo droll to fee the punchy little man thus playing the fool! And as for my fifter, who was peeping over the banifters, I thought fhe would have expired with laughter. However, at laft my father got tired of the man's buffoonery, particularly as all the fervants were in hearing, fo out of the houfe Mr Smith was marched in charge of the lads.

Now comes the beft part of this abfurd hiftory; for, in the morning, my ftep-father

received the moſt inſolent, violent letter, to the
effeᶜt, "that the insult offered to him, a gentleman, and member of a family who could
trace their anceſtry from—oh, dear! I forget
the man's folly—William the Conqueror, I
think centuries back, demanded the penalty
of blood to waſh out ſuch a foul ſtain on his
eſcutcheon ; that he ſhould feel degraded by
remaining in the neighbourhood of thoſe who
were in no way his equals ; ſo that, however
much he ſhould ever adore 'The Flower of
Armadale,' yet his honour was even dearer
to him than love. He ſhould go direᶜt to
his native country in the Weſt of England,"
naming the town, "where he would be
ready to fight either or both of the Armadale gentlemen, with piſtol or sword."

Of this elegant epiſtle, which in joke I
ſaid ought to have been framed in glaſs, of
courſe no notice was taken, except that of
amuſing us moſt exceſſively. We never ſaw
or heard of Mr Smith from that day to this ;

Bounce.

but we often laugh over Annabella's love adventure, which at the time afforded ſo much merriment to our large circle of re-lations, and John Kingſburgh, Allan's brother, ever regretted not having witneſſed the fun.

Wooed.

But it was not long after this affair that I had to meditate deeply on a ſubjeƈt which, involving, as it did, ſo completely my life's happineſs, the recolleƈtion is fraught with intereſt on the page of memory even at this diſtant date.

Our intimacy with the Kingſburgh family, and my friendſhip with dear Anne, then happily ſettled at Strathaird, who often had me to ſtay with her and delight myſelf with her little ones, was the means of my being more than ever in the ſociety of her favourite brother; therefore, no ſurpriſe was expreſſed—nay, on the contrary, the warmeſt ſatiſfaƈtion—when the faƈt of my engagement with Allan M'Donald became generally known; and joy it was to me, now that every feeling of reſtraint, ſo natural to be exiſting in the heart of a woman while uncertain if her regard is mutual, had paſſed away, to give place to the fulleſt confidence in converſation, to be aſſured that our affection had been reciprocated for a long time, although he deemed it beſt to be ſilent until he had a comfortable home to offer me. I now felt his ſilence on the ſubject was prudent on his part, and honourable towards myſelf.

Engaged.

His kind father, knowing his wiſhes, gave him poſſeſſion of a ſmall property ſituated on the eaſt ſide of Trotterniſh, on Lord M'Donald's eſtate. It was called Flodigary, a place I had often ſeen, yet little thought it would ever be my reſidence.

However, the marriage was delayed until the houſe was thoroughly in order, there was ſo much to do in the way of furniſhing and other expenſes, towards which I con-

tributed the greater part of my Jacobite fortune.

Half-pay.

Allan had attained the rank of Captain in the 84th Regiment, and preferring a quiet Highland life to the buſtle of a military one, he retired on half-pay. As for myſelf, my reminiſcences of England were not ſo agreeable as to cauſe a wiſh to return to it. No; on this ſubjeƈt we both felt alike, being contented to remain in the circle of attached relations and friends who had known us both when we both were wee little bodies.

My narrative now arrives to the end of 1750, when, on the 6th of November, I became a happy bride.

The wedding was numerouſly attended, every one looked bright and cheerful,—my loved mother and warm-hearted ſtep-father doing the honours of the well-ſpread table with true Highland hoſpitality. My happineſs was alſo increaſed by the affeƈtion evinced for me by every member of my huſband's family.

I was fo warmly welcomed into their circle, it cheers my heart even now to think of that brighteſt of all days within my recollection.

The muſic which I copy into this little ſtory of my ſayings and doings will perhaps ſurpriſe you, Maggie; but I will tell you all about it. It is a ditty I wrote myſelf years ago, at the time I was ſo intereſted in Prince Charles, and the tune alſo came into my head; but I never made it public until, on the day of my marriage, a requeſt came in the name of all the gueſts, that I would ſing it, ſo I was obliged to do ſo. Some years after, an Engliſh lady heard of it, and aſked my leave to write down the tune as I warbled it in my ſimple way, by which means the air has been preſerved, for I was not clever enough to write down muſical notes of any kind.

So now I have given the hiſtory of my little ſong, to which I ſhould not have alluded had I not been writing about my wedding. I hear, and certainly with ſurpriſe, that the

The ſong.

lady introduced it into England, where it has attained a kind of popularity, as being the humble production of "The Prince's Pre-ferver."

Original.

Lively, with energy.

Hie to the Highlands.

Oh! hie to the Highlands, my lad-die,

Be wel-comed by hearts warm and true, For

there's where ye'll fee, my ain lad-die, The

tar - tans and bon - nets of   blue.

And lift when they tell ye, my lad - die, Their

1st verse.

va - li - ant deeds of re - nown, Of

bat-tles they've fought for Prince Char - lie, The

true - born   heir   to   the Crown.   Oh!

II.
Ye'll hear of the chieftains of old,
Thofe fons of valour and worth;
But Charlie's own favourite clan was
M'Donald! the pride of the North!
    Oh! hie to the Highlands, &c.

III.
Ye'll meet with the laffies fae bonnie,
I fear ye will love them too well;
But heed not their fmiles, my ain laddie—
Your love I'll keep all to myfel.
    Oh! hie to the Highlands, &c.

After our marriage, we were a great deal at
Kingſburgh; indeed, my father and mother-
in-law were always kind to me, and even at
this diſtance of time, I cannot charge my
memory with a word of diſcord having paſſed
between us. The proverb in our country of Harmony.
"happy the wife that 's married to a mother-
leſs ſon," was not a matter of experience on
my part. I have a vivid recollection of dear
old Mrs M'Donald's bright ſmile of welcome,
when, in after-years, and ſurrounded by a
group of darling children, I found time to
go over to Kingſburgh. Allan was equally
pleaſed to have his parents at Flodigary; ſo,
thus contented and happy in ourſelves, my
wedded life glided on as peacefully as the
unruffled lake for many years, no particular
event occurring worthy of notice.

Our domeſtic circle was added to by the
marriages of my brother and John Kingſburgh,
—the former to an amiable girl, a M'Donald,
diſtantly related to us, and the latter choſe his

wife while vifiting a family in South Uift.
They both had children, who often were with
mine at Flodigary.   Oh! the noife of their
merry voices I have now in my head; to which
was combined the fcreaming of worthy Katie,
who was never fo much in her element as
when nurfing the bairns of her beloved " Mifs
Flora." She never called me otherwife, honeft
creature! and go wherever I might, fhe would
accompany me.   On fuch occafions the wee
bodies were completely a fecondary confider-
ation to her.

I remember Katie was my companion on
an occafion which is deeply impreffed on my
memory; indeed, the recollection of what I
am about to relate caufes me a fhudder of
horror.   Yes, it was a dreadful fcene!

We had fome friends in a dreary part of
the Highlands, who fcarcely ever left home,
but were accuftomed to enliven the folitude
of a habitation in a village that could only
boaft of a few fcattered huts for the poor

fishers and their half-starved families, by
inviting friends to stay for months at a time.
Most hospitable they were, yet they were
more pleased to welcome guests than were
the visitors to remain long in such a dull
house. I went there once when a girl, and
determined not to repeat the visit; but my
parents went frequently, being on most intimate terms; and once a letter from Mr
Douglas being received by my mother, saying
he hoped she would immediately come to
his wife, who was far from well, and wanted
her society, my mother entreated me to go
in her place, for she could not then leave
Armadale conveniently, and as she agreed
to look after the bairns and other matters,
Katie and I started on this duty visit.

When arrived and domesticated with these
kind people, it was a difficult concern to get
away. However, when Mrs Douglas was
sufficiently recovered to afford a loophole of
escape, I did contrive to gain a reluctant con-

Dull.

fent to our departure; and it was on our homeward journey an adventure occurred that I fhall never forget—I wifh I could.

The diftance between Burnfhiel and Armadale obliged me to fleep on the road, fo I ftopped for the night at a miferable low kind of inn, if fuch a hovel was worthy of being fo called. I had arranged that Katie fhould continue her journey with the boy driving the little Highland cart and luggage, and I was to follow the next day on horfeback with a guide, for I felt too tired to go on without reft. As for the honeft girl, it was the fame to her whether fhe jogged on by night or by day; fo, after partaking of food, which fhe and the lad feemed to relifh, off they went, leaving me in the only decent bedroom in the houfe. This room was over the kitchen, which I foon found out from the puffs of fmoke down the chimney, as well as the voices of men below.

I did not fee a woman about, and believe

An inn.

two men only were in attendance, for one of them fhowed me into the room, and brought my fupper.

It was a gloomy place to be alone in, for the high road was at fome diftance from the heath on which the inn ftood. The night, although dry, was chilly, and gufts of wind fhook the old window-frames, one of which I kept open to let out the fmoke.

Not feeling fleepy, or inclined to try the untempting-looking bed, I thought it a good opportunity to write a letter to our kind friend and relation, Sir Alexander M'Kenzie of Delvin; fo taking writing materials from a fmall box I ufually carried in my hand, *The box.* and feated in a corner as far as poffible from door or window, I got on as well as the light of a tallow-candle would allow of.

All this time the men were talking earneftly, in Gaelic, of courfe, when it feemed to me as if there was a kind of dif-pute, for one of them fpoke in a higher

The plot.

tone, and a word or two I overheard rather alarmed me; fo I foftly opened the door, and went to the ftair-head. They talked in a fort of whifper, but fright opened my ears to hear clearly enough that thefe villains were only waiting until they thought I was afleep, to enter the room and get poffeffion of the letter-box, which they expected contained money or valuables.

"And if," faid one of the ruffians, "fhe is likely to be troublefome, we know how to filence her—the fame as the laft. Ah! that was like to be a bad job, wafn't it?"

Oh! how can my horror be defcribed? Thank God I did not fcream, or make the leaft found; my feet feemed rooted to the ground, and yet the neceffity for immediate flight flafhed on my mind. In a fecond a plan of efcape was formed. I foftly clofed the door, and in ftooping to draw off my noify boots, oh, horror! what did I fee? A ftream of blood flowly oozing from under the bed, which made me raife the valance—*a dead body !*—a man apparently recently murdered !

A faint ficknefs came over me; I feared becoming infenfible; but offering up a few words of fervent prayer for help from that bleffed fource of ftrength in every danger, I haftily tore off the fheets and blanket, knotted them firmly together, and tied one end to the bed-poft, as fecurely as my poor trembling hands could do it. The other end I paffed over the fill of the window, which, thank God, was open; caught up my writing-box and fmall linen bundle, gently mounted the window-fill, and feizing hold of the fheets, which I prayed God might fupport my weight, flid down to the ground. Fortunately I landed on foft heather, fo not a found was heard. I had taken the precaution of blowing out the candle, that the vile men might have more trouble, on entering the room in the dark, to feel about for their intended victim, who trufted to be a mile or two

The rope.

on her road before her departure was difcovered!

The cold and frefh air revived me; fright
was as wings to my feet; for although long
after midnight, and too dark to fee a ftep
before me, I paced on, nearly running, and
frequently ftumbling over thofe pieces of
ftone which are generally on moffy ground.
It was a great exertion for a female no longer
young, befides being fo nervous; one might
have heard the beatings of my poor heart.

A couch.

At laft I came upon a ftone-dyke, which, on
climbing over, I found was a boundary-wall
from the high road.   This was fome comfort,
and alfo afforded me a reft; fo drawing my
warm cloth cloak clofer around me, and half
reclining on the fmall bundle, I actually fell
afleep! really afleep, Maggie.   Here I muft
have refled for fome hours, for on being
awoke by the rufhing found of a neighbouring
burn, the dawn was breaking fufficiently for
me to find my way on,—but whether on the

road to my home, was a myſtery time only would ſolve.

The clear water waſhing the ſparkling pebbles was tempting to the poor foot-ſore wanderer, ſo I drew from my bundle a leathern cup, which always journeyed with me, and was rendered ſacred in my eſtimation from its having touched the lips of the bonnieſt Prince in the world, and took a draught of the freſh water, then trudged onwards, tired and jaded; yet the ſight of the dawn gradually riſing from behind the hills, the ſtreaks of gray and pink-red, ſo often ſeen in early morn, which appeared to kiſs the high dark mountain peaks, was ſo enchanting, I thought neither of the chilly air nor of my troubles.

The ſight of a young red-haired laſſie croſſing a field to milk ſome cows, cheered me with the hopes of getting a draught of it ; ſo, at the coſt of a few bawbees, I was much refreſhed; alſo glad to be told that a village

The cup.

was not far off, where I fhould be able to get a fharry-dan to take me home. The girl feemed curious to know more, but I only afcertained from her what I wifhed to find out—where the Manfe was fituated, and the name of the Minifter. My reafon for feeing him, was to tell the ftrange adventure; alfo that inquiries might be inftituted relative to my dreadful difcovery, which might lead to the murderers being brought to juftice.

One of the wretches I could have fworn to if required; but, at all events, the thought ftruck me of informing the Minifter, who would act as he judged beft in the matter.

However, it was yet too early to knock up the family at the Manfe, fo after the girl had done with the cows, fhe conducted me to a fmall, rather tidy looking bothy, where her mother was buftling about, preparing the bairns' porridge. The good woman made me welcome, and truly glad was I to have a fhare of it, and a reft for my wearied limbs.

No doubt fhe was curious about me, but I did not enlighten her, or indeed care what fhe thought. I fimply faid I had bufinefs at the Manfe.

After an hour or two, the woman fent one of her children to fhow me the way. A refpectable looking elderly man was in the garden, overlooking a boy who was at work. This perfon I concluded was the minifter, fo I told him the horrid tale, and hoped he would kindly act a friendly part towards me.

On hearing my name he expreffed much intereft, having heard fuch wonderful things of my poor fimple felf years agone. He promifed to have the affair inveftigated by a friend of his, who was a Juftice of the Peace.

I was introduced to the ladies of his family at their hofpitable breakfaft-table, and they all praifed me for the courage I had fhown in my night adventure.

The Manfe.

Friends.

Moſt kind they were, wiſhing me to reſt a few days, and ſend a line to my huſband of what had occurred; but I was impatient to continue my journey; ſo, as ſoon as arrangements could be made, a Highland car with a driver who knew the road, for I was miles out of the direct way home, was at the gate, and I bade farewell to this amiable family, whoſe acquaintance, commencing under ſuch ſtrange circumſtances, has ripened into an intimacy that will, I hope, ever continue. The old man is dead, but the wife and daughters, now living in the village, the Manſe being occupied by another miniſter, we ſometimes go and viſit. You have heard me often ſpeak of them, Maggie,—the Gunns, formerly of Tweedale Manſe.

I wiſhed to get home, for when the excitement of danger, which had braced up my nervous ſyſtem, had paſſed off, I felt a languor coming over me, that might rapidly increaſe, and longed for complete reſt.

Oh ! it appeared an endlefs journey ! At laft, however, home was reached in fafety. My dear hufband's open arms received me with his ufual affection and anxious inquiries as to the caufe of delay. I had juft ftrength to tell him briefly what had happened, when I fainted and loft all recollection for above two hours.

I was for days in bed, fuffering from the fatigue and expofure from the cold of that dreadful, never-to-be-forgotten night of horror, which even now I hate to call to mind; fo fhall finifh the tragic tale by merely ftating, that Mr Gunn's friend was moft active in tracing out the fcene of the murder, making minute inquiries after the two men, but the wretches had decamped, leaving the evidence of their crime in the houfe, being, it was fuppofed, too hurried to inter their unfortunate victim, nor was it ever difcovered who he was.

The inn has been pulled down, which from

that day no one would occupy, for, of courfe, it was faid to be haunted. On our vifits to Burnfhiel, I always fhudder on paffing the fpot.

About the year 1766 there was brought to our diftant world news from abroad which was of intereft, for it informed us of Prince Charles's father, James III. of England, having died at the end of December 1765, at the age of feventy-eight. He had long been ailing, and unable to leave his refidence in Rome for three years; fo in our hearts we confidered our Prince as King Charles III.; but our informant went on to ftate that he was never liked at the Papal Court, being fufpected of having become a Proteftant, termed by the Romanifts, a heretic; but whether he is fo or not, his pretenfions are not likely to be acknowledged by the Pope.

He and his brother Prince Henry, Cardinal York, are not on cordial terms, poffibly for this reafon, that the Cardinal, as a ftanch

Charles III.

Romaniſt, could not, confiſtently with his high clerical poſition, fanction a wavering in the religious tenets of the Prince. Our friend told us that the latter is living in or near Florence.

Herefy.

No occurrence of any family importance interrupted our uſual quiet mode of life, ſo I paſs over a good many years, during which time our children were growing fine lads and laſſies; for between the dates of 1751 and 1766, we had ſeven olive branches ſporting around us, all born at Flodigary. They were named Charles, Ann, Alexander, Ranald, James, John, and my youngeſt, little Fanny. I am rather ſorry now that neither of my daughters were called after me. Let us hope in due time the name of Flora will be remembered, and that it may become a common family-name.

Alas! the next change in our domeſtic circle brought great ſorrow to my huſband and myſelf—the death of his dear father; by

which event Kingſburgh Houſe becoming
Allan's property, we left Flodigary to reſide
in the family-manſion.

It was long before I could feel myſelf the
miſtreſs of a houſe in which I had lived ſo
often as a gueſt. I thought much of years
gone by, and of the warm-hearted affection
ever ſhown me by my kind father-in-law;
a better man never exiſted. His death
occurred in 1772.

A curious circumſtance took place ſome-
where about this time. I do not preciſely
recollect the date, for I am now upwards of
ſixty-five, and at that age the memory begins
to have little holes which let ſlip ſuch ſundry
particulars. What I have to relate concerns
a wraith; ſo prick up your ſharp ears, dear
Maggie.

I was viſiting at our relations the
M‘Queens, when ſtaying there was a lady
whom I was told to notice, as ſhe had the
faculty of ſeeing ghoſts — real ſpirits,

Maggie! not only at night, but alfo in the daytime. At firft I was inclined to treat the fubject jokingly, requefting Mrs M'Queen would afk her not to give a fpecimen of her accomplifhment while I was in the houfe; but it was not long before a fact occurred which took away all the mirth I had indulged in.

This lady, Mrs M'Queen, a young laffie, alfo a vifitor, and myfelf, were fitting around a cofy fire in the bedroom of our kind hoftefs. Suddenly the lady gently touched Mrs M'Queen on the fhoulder, faying, in a low voice, "Turn round, and tell me who is ftanding by the drawers."

Eerie.

We all looked: I faw nothing, but heard the ruftle of a filk drefs, at the fame time a whiff of air feemed to pafs clofe to me, caufing a cold fhuddering fenfation I had never felt before.

Mrs M'Queen, ftarting up, put out her hand, and welcomed fome one by name;

then fhe fcreamed, crying out that it was a fpirit, for the young lady had faintly fmiled and difappeared, "as if fhe funk into the ground."

That was her defcription of this ftrange affair. The little girl faw nothing, nor did fhe feel the chilling puff of wind. She laughed at us, faying it was all nonfenfe. However, I relate fimply what occurred, fo people may judge for themfelves. Perhaps many would be inclined to think it was an illufion of a vivid imagination; yet as certain

Fact.

I am of a fpectre having appeared in that room as that I am now writing thefe lines; and a further proof was given of Mrs M'Queen's not having been miftaken, by the arrival of a letter fome days later from a relation of the young lady, who mentioned that her fifter had died precifely at the time the fpirit appeared in Mrs M'Queen's bedroom.

Although by no means a nervous perfon, yet I avoided that room ever after.

Sometime in the year 1773—I forget the exact date—Kingsburgh House received no less a personage than the great Doctor Samuel Johnson, he having brought a letter of introduction. from one of my former London friends. He was accompanied by Mr Boswell, an intimate companion, whom he called "Bosey;" and the purport of their visit to the Highlands was to make up a book, to be printed, with all the wonders they saw in our simple country. Of course the greatest of those wonders was the once celebrated "Miss Flora." So after listening with becoming gravity to the flattering praises of the talented Doctor, I promised him the gratification of resting for the night in our guest-room, in which was the bed with the tartan hangings rendered so precious to us as having been slept in by the dear Prince.

Doctor Johnson remarked afterwards, that the ambitious thoughts he had anticipated from sleeping in a bed occupied, as he expressed

Notes.

it, " by the laft of the Stuarts," did not
trouble his repofe. On taking leave, I faid
how honoured I felt by his vifit ; which little
piece of civility, added to our humble fhow
of hofpitality to himfelf and friend, muft have
pleafed the old gentleman, for he afterwards
wrote very polite things of me in his printed
book, and as he greatly difliked Scotch people,
a fentiment eafily difcerned in his converfation,
befides being rather a woman-hater, I confidered myfelf moft particularly favoured.

It is fingular how frequently the clevereft
perfons are addicted to queer habits ! Why, this
Doctor Johnfon, this man of deep learning,
never entered a room without placing his right
foot over the door-fill, and if by forgetfulnefs
the left chanced to prefent itfelf, he would
retire a few fteps to enable the guilty member
to act with propriety ! He gave as a reafon
" that better luck attended the right than the
left."

Oh, moft fapient Doctor ! you were wrong

to ridicule Scotch people and their fuper-
ftitions. But certainly he wrote moft clever
books.

So much for Dr Johnfon's vifit to Kingfburgh, nor was I forry to have feen the man
whom all the world fpoke of as being the
greateft fcholar of the age.

In 1775 my hufband put in practice a plan
he and I had often talked over—that of joining the emigrants who were leaving their native
hills, to better their fortunes on the other
fide of the Atlantic.

We were induced to favour this fcheme,
more particularly as a fucceffion of failures
of the crops, and unforefeen family expenfes, | Hard times.
rather cramped our fmall income. So, after
making various domeftic arrangements, one
of which was to fettle our dear boy Johnnie
under the care of a kind friend, Sir Alexander
M'Kenzie of Delvin, near Dunkeld, until he
was of age for an India appointment, we took
fhip for North America. The others went

with us, my youngeſt girl excepted, whom I left with friends: ſhe was only nine years old.

Ann was a fine young woman, and my ſons as promiſing fellows as ever a mother could deſire.

Believe me, dear Maggie, in packing the things, the Prince's ſheet was put up in lavender, ſo determined I was to be laid in it, whenever it might pleaſe my Heavenly Father to command the end of my days.

On reaching North Carolina, Allan ſoon purchaſed and ſettled upon an eſtate, but our tranquillity was ere long broken up by the diſturbed ſtate of the country; and my huſband took an active part in that dreadful War of Independence. The Highlanders were now as forward in evincing attachment to the Britiſh Government as they had furiouſly oppoſed it in former years.

My poor huſband, being loyally diſpoſed, was treated harſhly by the oppoſite party, and was confined for fome time in gaol at Halifax.

After being liberated, he was officered in a loyal corps, the North Carolina High-landers; and although America fuited me and the young people, yet my hufband thought it advifable, at the conclufion of the war, to quit a country that had involved us in anxiety and trouble almoft from the firft month of our landing on its fhores. So, at a favourable feafon for departure, we failed for our native country, all of us, excepting our fons Charles and Ranald, who were in New York expecting appointments, which they foon after obtained: Alexander was already, dear boy, at fea. Thus our family was reduced in number.

On the voyage home, all went on well until the veffel encountered a French fhip of war, and we were alarmed on finding that an action was likely to take place. The Captain gave orders for the ladies to remain

Situations.

below, fafe from the fkirmifh; but I could
not reft quiet, knowing my hufband's fpirit
and energy would carry him into the thick
of the fighting, therefore I rufhed up the
companion-ladder, I think it was fo called,
and infifted on remaining on deck to fhare
my hufband's fate, whatever that might be.

Well, dear Maggie, thinking the failors
were not fo active as they ought to have
been—and they appeared creftfallen, as if they
expected a defeat—I took courage, and urged
them on by afferting their rights and the cer-
tainty of victory. Alas! for my weak en-
deavours to be of fervice I was badly rewarded,
being thrown down in the noife and confufion
on deck, I was fain to go below, fuffering
excruciating agony in my arm, which the
Doctor, who was fortunately on board, pro-
nounced to be broken. It was well fet, yet
from that time to this, it has been confider-
ably weaker than the other. So you fee I
have perilled my life for both the Houfes of

Loyal.

Stuart and Brunſwick, and gained nothing from either ſide!

On our return to Skye we were warmly welcomed by a hoſt of relations and dear friends; yet, alas! many a gap there was in the family circle. Death had been rife on our native hills, and ſincerely we had to mourn the loſs of ſeveral valued friends. My dear mother and my dear relations at Kingſ-burgh had long gone to their reſt, even before we went to America.

Welcome.

There was alſo a change at Strathaird, for my ſiſter-in-law, Anne M'Aliſter, having become a widow, in due time remarried with M'Kinnon of Corrychatachan, a widower with a family; and one of his ſons formed an attachment to a daughter of Anne's, which ultimately led to a marriage.

Mrs M'Kinnon has had no family in her ſecond marriage. She was a dear creature, and made as good and amiable a wife at Corry as ſhe had done while at Strathaird;

indeed, fhe was a kind fifter-in-law, whom I loved moft dearly.

There was another link added to our chain of family relationfhip, by a marriage at Cuid-rach between my fifter Annabella's fon, a fine young man, Donald M‘Donald, and my dear Fanny, our youngeft daughter. This union afforded my hufband and myfelf much fatif-faction. How proud we were of Fanny—fhe was fuch a fine young woman! "Hey, ma'am, fhe's juft a magnificent cretur!" as an old Highland laird ftyled my darling girl. She was very young, fcarcely out of childhood, when Donald took her from us, and never have we repented giving her to fuch a good amiable man.

One of my nieces, a daughter of Annabella, fettled at Courthill, having married her coufin, Major M‘Donald, all thefe intermarriages formed a ftrong band of family affection, creating a feeling of intereft which, while our enemy Time wears on, is increafed inftead of

Son-in-law.

being diminifhed. In only one fenfe, perhaps, is the bond rendered more painful,—when coufins happy in married life are fevered by the ftream of death. This I have had to witnefs in many cafes.

In this catalogue of family-weddings that of my eldeft daughter, Anne, to Major M'Leod, was entirely with the fanction of her parents; a more excellent worthy hufband fhe could not have found anywhere. She has now a group of interefting children; and indeed, at the time I write this, my return home from attending her during one of her confinements is very recent. My daughters keep Grannie's time pretty well occupied by having to take thefe journeys, which remind me of our family fymbol, " *Per mare per terras,*" for fome one Motto. told me that thefe words Englifhed mean " By fea and by land,"—the origin of which fentence I will explain, dear Maggie, by inferting here the Highland legend attaching to it.

In the early days of Scotland's ftate of bar-

barifm, when our anceftors had no fixed laws
to govern their favage actions, when might was
right, and daily conflicts occurred for the poffeffion of unappropriated lands, the Ifland of
Skye was coveted by the chiefs of two clans:
one was a M'Donald; I have forgotten the
name of the other, it being long fince I read
the account.

After bitter hoftilities between thefe men,
each determined to obtain the ifland for himfelf and his pofterity, they agreed to fettle the
difpute in this manner.

A day was fixed, and friends of the combat-
ants appointed as umpires to decide the merits
of a boat-race; for the conditions were, that
whichever of the men firft reached the fhore,
the ifland was from that moment to belong
to him and his heirs.

It was a hard pull, and M'Donald's antago-
nift had every profpect of fuccefs, when fud-
denly our anceftor feized a hatchet, chopped
off his arm, in the hand of which was the crofs

Teft.

crofflet, this conflict taking place in the time of the Crufades, and flinging it with the force of a favage on the fhore, exclaimed, "M'Donald has gained; his flefh has firft touched the land!'

This, dear Maggie, was the origin of our motto, and fince thofe favage times the Ifle of Skye has been in the poffeffion of the M'Donalds. Origin.

I often think of "fea and land" on my interefting family journeys; for on the occafion of being fummoned by my eldeft daughter, I have far to go to crofs the water, and my youngeft is fettled very far inland.

I do not expect to fee much of our fons, for having chofen their profeffions, they will find a difficulty in obtaining leave to' vifit Scotland. Alas! dear Maggie! you know the affliction I and his father were in, on learning the fad tale of our dear fon Sandie, who was loft at fea—fwept off the deck in a violent ftorm. It cut me to the heart; he was fuch a noble fpirited lad—oh! how dear to me!

We have good accounts of the others, all doing well, and are, by what we hear, much liked in their regiments. Charles has his captaincy in the "Queen's Rangers." Ranald is alfo a Captain in the Marine fervice: he is the handfomeft of all my fons. James is now ferving in Tarlton's Britifh Legion; and from our dear John, now in India at Fort Marlbro', we receive the moft dutiful, fenfible letters. He has it in his power to fhow his talents, being in the Engineering department of the Eaft India Service. Not only was he educated at the High School of Edinburgh, but he alfo had the advantage of his claffics being attended to while under the care of kind M'Kenzie of Delvin, who made him work at his books during the holiday-time, which I believe Mafter Johnnie did not much relifh, yet now he will find the benefit of it. Indeed, he often expreffes a

grateful feeling for the worthy old gentleman, who, as my fon fays, meant well by
urging on his ftudies, although a young lad
might be excufed, if he fhowed a difinclina-
tion to turn out of a warm bed on cold
winter mornings, to pore over Latin and
Greek exercifes, efpecially during the few
weeks ufually fpent in home-recreation.

Johnnie told me he never fhould forget
Sir Alexander M'Kenzie's daily habit of
aroufing him before daylight, with the fame
Latin fentence dunned into his ears every
morning, fomething about "the Mufes being
early rifers." However, whether they were
fo or not, Johnnie did not care, and only had
the boyifh feeling of vexation at having his
reft difturbed; but now he can eftimate the
kindnefs of the old gentleman, and has often
written to him from India.

John has a fenfible face, with fine ex-
preffive eyes, otherwife he is not fo good-look-
ing as his elder brothers. Ranald is, as I faid

before, exceedingly handſome, and Charles is
a ſplendid fellow, on whoſe appearance my
huſband and I have been complimented by
Lord M‘Donald, with whom he is a great
favourite.

Proud.

Am I a vain mother, Maggie ? If you, and
other readers of these pages conſider me ſo,
I crave forgiveneſs on the ſcore of maternal
affeⳤion.

Yes ; I am proud of all my children ;
and when together in the family-circle, none
of them can feel more cheerful than the
" auld mither " in her arm-chair.

Ranald is eſpecially plucky, as the lads
ſay, about his adventures, having been with
Rodney at the taking of St Euſtatia. When
on that ſubjeⳤ he rides the high horſe to
perfeⳤion, and gives ſuch a graphic account
of the engagement, that we get moſt inter-
ested in liſtening to him.

And next to my own family, every member
of whom is ſo entwined in the cords of my

heart, there is yet one object to intereſt my feelings of friendly regard—the one for whom I ſuffered in early life ſo much miſery and anxiety of mind. You know, Maggie, to whom I allude, to our own dear Prince, now in a foreign land, at this time reſiding near Florence under the title of the Count of Albany.

His brother, Cardinal York, is in Rome, and it was only lately my huſband and I had intelligence of them, which was in conſequence of a converſation that occurred between the Cardinal and a Highland gentleman, not very long ſince, relative to myſelf.

It ſeems the Cardinal, knowing he was from the Iſle of Skye, made inquiries as to what had become of the young Highland lady who had ſo courageouſly aided his brother in eſcaping from his enemies? And then added, that he did not know in what circumſtances I might be, but that—mind the condition, Maggie!—if I would change my

Albany.

creed, and become a Romaniſt, he would offer me a penſion yearly, for any ſum I liked to name.

My friend, judging rightly as to the ſtate of my religious feelings, took upon himſelf to decline ſuch a propoſal, reſpectfully adding, that I did not require pecuniary aid; even if I did, he was certain the offer, with ſuch a condition attached, would be conſidered the reverſe of a compliment in the caſe of a perſon who is, as well as each of her family, a ſtanch Proteſtant. No; had I been ſtarving, I would not have accepted the Cardinal's favour. Yet I believe his Royal Highneſs meant kindly; ſo, viewing the matter in that light, he has my thanks and gratitude for the recollection of a ſimple body in a far-off country.

Indeed, Prince Henry's inquiry after me ſhowed more thoughtfulneſs than has been evinced by Prince Charles, or rather, our Sovereign, for ſuch he now is, who up to the preſent time, I am told, has not once aſked whether I am dead or alive, or ever alluded to his " Preferver."

I underftand he has married a foreign Princefs, young enough to be his daughter, and that, like all matches contracted between perfons where there exifts a great difparity in age, it has turned out very unhappily.

In 1772.

Poor unfortunate Prince! What a fad fate is his! How painful muft be his thoughts when memory traces back the hills and dales of Scotland, and the devoted band of faithful Highlanders who bled and died for his fake! Nay, fo peculiarly fenfitive is he on this fubject, that on the occafion of a Scotch gentleman being honoured by an invitation to dinner, the converfation turning on the Battle of Culloden, and the brave conduct of his foldiery, his Royal Highnefs was fo agitated, he fell down in a fit, on which a lady, faid to be a very near relation, who refided with him, came hurriedly into the room. " Ah, Sir!" faid fhe, " you muft have touched on a forbidden fubject: the Prince is always fo excited when allufion is made to Scotland and the Highlanders. I muft requeft you will not venture on it again !"

Alas! poor Charlie! He is, in all probability, fated to be the laft of the Stuarts.

We Highlanders confider him now as our legal Sovereign, Charles III. of Scotland and England, his father, King James, having, as I faid before, died in 1765; but I hear he is only thus acknowledged abroad by his friends and dependants.

Charles III.

Alas! he may not laft long, being feeble and fadly broken-down in fpirits. His chief amufement is mufic, of which he is paffionately fond; and many of his evenings are paffed with a mufician named Corri, who plays the harpfichord, and the Prince the violincello.

Alfo, his Royal Highnefs is a good compofer of fongs and all forts of mufic.

People do fay that within the laft few years

he has fometimes vifited England under a
feigned name; but whether fuch a report be
true or falfe, he has never reached the Highlands. No; if he had ever come to our blue
hills he could not have concealed himfelf,
the warmth of our hearts would have found
him out, dear perfecuted Prince!

My ftep-father was told that at a public
affemblage of Highland and Englifh gentlemen, the Prince being prefent, he was fo
much affected at hearing a young Highlander
fing the old pathetic ballad of "Lochaber
no more," he was obliged to leave the room;
he was in tears. How he is belied by the
many who ftate that Prince Charles is want-
ing in feeling! Quite the reverfe; he is only
too fenfitive; and they are no true friends
who make any allufion to Scotland before
him.

But how my pen does run on! I am
furprifed at myfelf. Really it is full time I
fhould finifh filling up fo many quires of

Senfitive.

letter-paper,—I believe the greater part of the ſtock-in-trade of the worthy grocer, who alſo deals in ſtationery, in the adjoining village. Perhaps he is under the deluſion that I am plotting againſt the Government in my old age, for he gazes with aſtoniſhment when "the leddy at the big houſe" ſo frequently purchaſes from his laſt inveſtment; and as for my huſband, his good-humoured ſmile comes over his bonny old face when, on entering the room, he ſees me occupied in "dotting down," as you called it, Maggie, the recollections of former days.

Giving way to the memory is like opening the flood-gate of a ruſhing ſtream: its power cannot be checked; nay, it is even added to by the force of the waters it meets with in its courſe. So is it with this MS., which on commencing I intended ſhould only extend to a few pages, but my mind has been arouſed, as if from a ſleepy dream of the paſt, to exert its dormant powers in an

Suſpicions.

humble endeavour to exercife a ufually flug-
gifh pen, for the pleafure of being enabled
to intereft my friends by a perufal of that
which, I can affure.them, has alfo interefted
me in the writing.

It is true much that is painful has, as in
a picture, been brought out in vivid colours
to my mind's eye, yet, at the fame time, here
and there the picture of my life is interfperfed
with dafhes of happy recollections, which even
now cheer the heart of the "auld Highland
mither." The rainbow fucceeding a fhower
is a pleafing fight, but my contentment is
equally bright, and lefs evanefcent, than that
moft beautiful of Nature's works.

So now, having nothing more to add to
the many pages that perhaps fome of my
friends, who are too fincere to flatter me,
may truly confider had far better not have
been written, I have only to fay good-bye to
my little MS., which, having been originally
commenced for your edification, my dear

Evening.

young friend, after it has gone the round of my relations, and afforded them a few hours' amuſement in the peruſal, I intend as a preſent to yourſelf, to do what you like with, for I never care to ſee it again.

While writing theſe laſt words, my huſband, who unknown to me was looking over my ſhoulder, ſtartled me by exclaiming, " Give it away, indeed! No; my dear wife ſhall do nothing of the kind: it ſhall never be parted with. So remember that I receive theſe papers into my own poſſeſſion after Maggie and the others who are clamouring to read them have ſatiſſied their curioſity. What- ever they may think, mind, dear Flory, the handwriting of one ſo dear to me ſhall never run the chance of being loſt or deſtroyed."

So, Maggie, what my lord and maſter ſays, I, like a good wife, muſt abide by. Therefore you muſt accept the inclination as the act; and pray take care of the MS., which it ſeems the laird of Kingſburgh ſo highly values. Poſſibly

Love.

he conſiders it will hereafter prove a ſplendid addition to the literature of our dear native Highlands!

You will perceive I finiſh this in my own home, but it was begun in your mother's pretty reſidence, where, if you recollect, Maggie, I was on a viſit when you firſt ſuggeſted the idea of my " dotting down" the curious circumſtances which have occurred in my life's journey of now ſixty-five years.

Your wiſh has been reſponded to. Farewell, dear girl! and that every preſent and future happineſs may be yours, is the ſincere and heartfelt deſire of your very affectionate old friend.

Good-bye.

                    FLORA M'DONALD.

KINGSBURGH HOUSE, 1787.

APPENDIX.

EDITORIAL.

———◇———

As the reader may feel interefted in the after-life of many perfons mentioned in the foregoing pages, the following particulars are added by the grand-daughter of the "Preferver of Prince Charles."

EDITORIAL AND SUPPLEMENTARY.

———◇———

FLORA M'DONALD retained to the laſt a great diſlike to hear alluſions made to the reigning monarch of England, nor would ſhe ever name George III. ; and on one occaſion ſhe not only very ſharply reprimanded her ſon John for ſtyling the latter "His Majeſty," but actually ſlapped the poor boy's face, ſaying, "ſhe would hear nothing of ' Soft Geordie.' "

Her life was paſſed in Skye, and at her death, which occurred the 5th March 1790, in her ſixty-ninth year, the ſheet ſhe had preſerved for ſo many years was uſed as her ſhroud. The ſheet

She was interred in the burial ground of

Kilmuir, in Trotternish, which enclosed the tombs of the Kingsburgh family.

The funeral was attended by three thousand persons, amongst whom were some of high rank, and refreshments were liberally provided.

Her youngest son, Lieutenant-Colonel John M'Donald, originally had a slab-stone to his mother's memory, on which were inscribed the suitable words of Dr Johnson, quoted in the title-page of this book, sent to Skye, but it has been utterly destroyed by tourists taking away pieces of the marble as relics.

In 1860 a great-grandson of Flora, Captain, now Major, John M'Donald, had another tombstone prepared to mark her last resting-place, with the following inscription :—

Epitaph.

" In the history of Scotland and England is recorded the name of her by whose memory this tablet is rendered facred; and mankind will confider that in FLORA M'DONALD were united the calm heroic fortitude of a man, together with the unfelfifh devotion of a woman. Under Providence fhe faved PRINCE CHARLES EDWARD STUART from death on a fcaffold, thus preventing the Houfe of Hanover incurring the blame of an impolitic judicial murder."

Flora M'Donald died in the houfe of a dear friend and relative, Mrs M'Queen of Penendoune, wife of the Minifter of Snizort, who lived not far from Kingfburgh.

Her hufband furvived her for two years. He died at Kingfburgh in 1792, and was interred at Kilmuir in Darinifh, Dunvegan.

All dead.

Their eldeft fon, Charles, was an elegant, accomplifhed man. He furvived his parents a few years; and at his funeral, his chief,

Lord M'Donald, on feeing the coffin lowered into the grave, turned to the mourners, and faid, "There lies the moft finifhed gentleman of my family and name." His Lordfhip was very partial to Captain Charles, and often received him at his houfe.

Charles and Ranald were unmarried. James married Amelia, a daughter of M'Donald of Skybofte. He had two fons, both in the Eaft India Company's fervice, and a married daughter. None are living.

John. John was twice married—firft in India to the widow of L. Bogle, Efq., and he had two children, who died in their infancy.

On his return to England, he married, fecondly, Frances Maria, eldeft daughter of the late Sir Robert Chambers, Chief-Juftice of Bengal, by whom he had a family of feven fons and two daughters, who are all deceafed, excepting his eldeft daughter—who edits this autobiography.

Ann, Mrs Major M'Leod, had a family. None are living.

Fanny, Mrs M'Donald of Cuidrach, had a family : all deceafed.

Many of the above-named grandfons and grand-daughters of Flora have married, and their children and grandchildren are numerous, and they can thus count four generations from their renowned anceftrefs. To give the names of all thefe defcendants would be beyond the limits of this little work.

Niel M'Donald M'Eachan, who accompanied Flora in the boat, eventually joined Prince Charles, and went with his Royal Highnefs to France.

At his royal mafter's requeft, Niel was

appointed a Lieutenant in Ogilvie's Regiment of the Scotch Brigade in the ſervice of France.

He married a French perſon, and his ſon, alſo in the army, became one of Napoleon I.'s greateſt Generals, Mareſchal M'Donald, Duc de Tarante.

Niel's ſon.

In one of Niel M'Eachan's letters, he mentioned that on the occaſion of Prince Charles being ignominiouſly treated by the French King, who had him ſent to the Caſtle of Vincennes, where he was placed in a ſhabby room, with no attendant but M'Eachan, he gave way to his wounded feelings. Throwing himſelf on a chair, he claſped his hands together, and burſt into tears. "Oh! my faithful mountaineers!" exclaimed he; "would I were ſtill with you!—I ſhould never have been thus inſulted!"

He wept bitterly, but not until alone with his faithful companion; for while the French officers and guards were prefent, his manner was dignified and lofty.

Prince Charles Edward Stuart, virtually King Charles, died in January 1788, in his fixty-eighth year. He was interred in the Cathedral of St Peter's in Rome. He had married in 1772 a German Princefs, Louifa Maximiliana Carolina of Stolberg-Guederan, from whom he feparated fhortly after. She was thirty-two years younger than himfelf. His widow furvived him nearly thirty-fix years, dying in January 1824. She was a warm friend and patronefs of the poet Alfieri, to whofe memory fhe erected a monument by Canova. She refided in Paris after leaving Prince Charles, but at the time of the French Revolution fhe returned to Florence; and after the death of Alfieri, fhe made a left-handed marriage with a French painter, Francis Xavier Fabre, who had been a friend of the poet.

Prince Charles had a daughter by a Mifs Walkinſhaw, whom he created Comteſſe d'Albany. She refided with him until his death, and he left her all his property.

George III., having heard that Henry Stuart, Cardinal York, was reduced in means owing to the firſt French Revolution, allowed his diſtreſſed royal relative four thouſand per annum, which penfion he enjoyed until his death in 1807, in his eighty-third year.

Henry IX.

By the death of Prince Charles, Prince Henry became entitled to his brother's rights refpecting the fovereignty of Great Britain, but he wifely made no attempt to gain the crown. On his death, he bequeathed, as Henry Stuart, to George IV., then Prince of Wales, the crown-jewels of his grand-father, James II., among which was included the Order of the Garter as worn by Charles I.

The Cardinal's death made George III. King by inheritance from the Stuarts, as previouſly he had inherited only from the Houſe of Hanover.

Over the remains of James III., Charles III., and Henry IX., Kings of England, a noble monument has been erected in St Peter's at Rome, at the expenſe of the Houſe of Hanover. The inſcription is as follows :—

JACOBO III.

JACOBO II. MAGNÆ BRIT : REGIS FILIO,

KAROLO EDWARDO,

ET HENRICO, DECANO PATRUM CARDINALIUM,

JACOBI III. FILIIS,

REGIÆ STIRPIS STUARDIÆ POSTREMIS,

ANNO MDCCCXIX.

————

BEATI MORTUI

QUI IN DOMINO MORIUNTUR.

LINES by Mrs GRANT of Laggan, *to* Colonel
JOHN M'DONALD, *the youngeſt ſon of*
" *Flora.*"

" Let those of wealth and empty titles proud
    Dazzle with idle pomp the vulgar crowd ;
    'Tis *thine* a nobler ancestry to boast
    For courage famed, for virtue honoured most.
    Calm fortitude in female graces drest
    Adorn'd the generous *Flora's* dauntless breast,
    With ev'ry milder charm that sweetens life, —
    The tender mother, and the virtuous wife, —
    And all that loyal truth and courage claim,
    Such honours deck the gentle heroine's name,
    Who now to thee bequeaths her well-won fame."

FLORA M^cDONALD :

*" A name that will be mentioned in hiſtory,
and if courage and fidelity be virtues, mentioned with honour.   She is a woman of
middle ſtature, ſoft features, gentle manners,
and elegant preſence."*

So wrote Dr Johnſon.